The Step-Doctors 2

Seeded by a Step

by

J.D. GRAYSON

28,000 words

CONTENTS

All books are now available in Paperback. For autographed copies please send your request to JDGrayson@hotmail.com

Visit J.D. Grayson's website to signup for a new release alerts.

Website: www.JDGraysonBooks.com

Twitter: @JDGraysonBooks

CHAPTER ONE

Ting, ting, ting, Dr. Sean Abel tapped his champagne glass with a spoon. Standing before a crowd of family members, he wore a pricy suit. His stepsister stood closely beside him, trembling in-place. Her fire-red dress clung to curves like a deadly mountain road. All eyes fixated upon them both. The doctor said, "I'd like to make an announcement."

Six months had passed since Darcy and Sean's relationship became official. Their chemistry got stronger with each moment, sexual passion burned hotter than molten lava. Lust grew into true love, leaving no doubt in their minds: it was time to unite in marriage.

Familiar smiles flashed around the lavish ballroom. It was the annual family reunion. Members of the large Abel clan filled every table in the ballroom. A tradition dating back years, it was a time to catch up on life's events and gossip. A memorable and anticipated event, the current year would be no exception.

Dr. Tim Abel sat at their table, awaiting the expected announcement. He was excited for them, though stressed. Darcy gazed over at her stepfather, unsure if nerves or sadness was glazing his eyes. At that moment, her own nerves were frayed. She warned herself, *Don't vomit on any of them! At least save it until after they're told! It will provide a distraction from the horror!*

The dark-haired, dapper Sean continued with his announcement. "I know many of you wondered when I'd finally man-up...exit bachelorhood. Well, I've finally found the cure."

"Awww," the room gushed and buzzed with excitement. "Who is she?" one member shouted. "Is she here?" yelled another.

Sean lifted his glass into the air. "Please join me in a champagne toast. Let us welcome to the family...actually, she's already *in* the family. My fiancé', Darcy Smith."

The room went dead silent. "Who's that?" A voice echoed throughout the room. "Dear lord...not his...*stepsister!*" said another family member's anguished voice.

Darcy's porcelain skin out shined her dress and hair. A sweating Sean turned to her. She waved at the crowd, numb from fear. *I think they're about to stone me. OK, they don't have stones...but they do have stale dinner rolls. That's just as deadly.*

A laugh echoed across the ballroom, another followed. "It's a joke. He's pulling our legs!" a voice shouted. More laughter joined in on the fun.

Sean grabbed Darcy's hand, holding up her ring finger. Reflected light hit the diamond, blinding their eyes like a sparkling sun. "It's true! I'm going to marry my STEPSISTER! I would've expected a little more class from my family."

"This is sacrilege!" yelled one.

"Gross!" shouted another.

"Three-headed children!" topped it all off. The crowd gasped in horror.

Fury filled Sean's face. "She's NOT blood relation!"

Some formed prayer circles, others shouted curses, a few began to cry. "Burn them at the stake...and I don't mean prime rib!" yelled drunken Uncle Rick.

Darcy whispered, "Sean...let's go. I'm gonna vomit!"

Sean was so fueled with anger he didn't even hear her plea. "Who the hell are you people to judge *us*? We have *actual* criminals, predators, and drug addicts in this family...in this room *tonight*! Shit, I happen to know some of you once voted for Jimmy Carter!"

An even greater gasp of horror filled the room, though no one dared admit such a shameful mistake. "I didn't vote for *him*! *They* did!" many shouted in defensiveness, pointing at other family members.

Sean continued, "You can overlook *those* offenses...but you'll judge me for who I love? It's legal, damn you!"

"Marrying your sister's sick!" drunken Uncle Rick shouted again, getting in Sean's face.

The young doctor's fist tightened, as he bumped chests with the man. Darcy stepped between the two. She tried to push nausea aside, attempting to defuse the situation. "Now, Uncle Rick...you know I'm his stepsister."

"You don't call me step-uncle!" Uncle Rick accused.

"What the hell does *that* prove?" Sean shouted.

"It's proof you're a degenerate! That you're a sicko!" Uncle Rick yelled.

"Yes, I'm really sick...like the vomit kinda sick," Darcy's soft voice evaporated in the shouting.

The two men screamed away, as Dr. Tim Abel rose from his seat. "Stop it now, Rick! You're my brother...they are your nephew and step-niece. You know better than this. You should be ashamed of yourself! In fact, you *all* should be ashamed!"

A hush came over the crowd. The respected doctor was not one to draw attention to himself. When he spoke, people listened. Tim continued, "This is legal...perfectly fine by every rule in the book. Yet, you sit in judgment...because it makes *you* uncomfortable. You all know...I lost the woman I loved...Darcy's mother...to unspeakable tragedy. I'd give my life to save her from that *scumbag*..." Tim paused before finishing. Looking over at Darcy, he remembered, *Watch your words...she doesn't know.* "Save her from the...*driver*...who hit her. You're lucky to find true love once in your life...step or no-step. Sean has *that* love for Darcy...they'll marry, and I'll be proud."

A smile crossed Sean's face, thankful for his father's support and courage. "Thanks, Dad. We're proud to call you *family*."

The two men nodded at each other. Tim Abel continued on. "And after that...I'll deliver their offspring...my grandchild! And if you people can't deal with that...then we'll take our family unit elsewhere!" He placed his napkin down, pulling out his chair to leave.

Before any move could be made, a drunk Uncle Rick asked, "Will all three heads get a name?" His obnoxious laugh filled the room, followed by others.

Sean's fists tightened, as he prepared to strike his uncle. However, Darcy struck first. *BLURRRRRRRLB!* A stream of projectile vomit sailed from her mouth, decorating Uncle Rick's face. All laughter stopped, as the Abel clan watched in sickened disbelief.

After the jackass uncle was drenched, Sean wiped Darcy's mouth with a cloth napkin. Proudly putting his arm around her, he stood firmly before his familial judges. Tim Abel placed his hands upon their shoulders, pulling them close. "Let's go home."

*****

"Do you, Darcy Smith, take Sean Abel to be your lawfully-wedded husband, to have and to hold from this day forward, for better, for worse, for richer, for poorer, in sickness and health, until death do you part?"

"I do," Darcy said sincerely. Her innocent smile beamed, eyes glazed with tears. Although she'd always imagined a fairytale wedding full of guests, none of that mattered anymore. One man held her heart, no fancy frills or decor could change that.

They stood in a beautiful old chapel. Mildewed stones constructed the walls, candles were lit along the sides, wooden beams formed a peaked ceiling, and a faded cross backed a carved alter. The pews were dusty, air musty, and an intimate glow of history warmed their skin.

Their only guest was Darcy's stepfather, standing behind the couple in support. It wasn't a pretentious show as many weddings are. The quickly maturing girl appreciated a very important fact: *This isn't a party...it's a commitment. It's not a room of fakes and drunks whispering gossip and hate...it's the people who matter to me. It's the people I love.*

The priest continued with the vows, turning towards Sean. "And do you, Sean Abel, take Darcy Smith to be your lawfully-wedded wife, to have and to hold from this day forward, for better, for worse, for richer, for poorer, in sickness and health, until death do you part?"

Sean turned to his stepsister, staring into her radiant blue eyes. His momentary silence was not hesitation, but admiration. "I do," he said proudly.

"Then I hereby pronounce you, man and wife, Mr. and Mrs. Abel. You may kiss your bride," the priest said.

Smiles crossed their faces. Moving in toward one another, they shared a passionate kiss. "Congratulations," Tim Abel said from behind.

Sean hugged his father, thankful for the man's support. Next, Tim hugged Darcy. He held her tight, almost desperately. *Is he trembling?* Darcy wondered. *Why? He sounds happy, but something's not right with him lately. Worse than usual.*

As the hug broke, Darcy stared beyond her stepfather's surface-smile. Gazing into his eyes, she saw the same pain which had always been. After their talk at the cemetery, she tried to believe he'd be alright. Though, her thoughts betrayed her willful ignorance. *It's about my mother. This probably reminds him of his own wedding. He still hurts...no matter what I tell myself. I just wish I could help him. I know it's not my fault my love didn't heal his pain. I wish I could heal his heart, help him love again...help him live again. If there was anything I could do...I'd do it.*

*****

The stunning stepsister-wife stood before her new husband. Inside their honeymoon suite, Sean watched in awe. Darcy's red hair lie upon her white satin dress. The two contrasted like fire and ice. Her strapless wedding gown form-fit to every delicious curves. If she had wings, an angel she'd be.

Sean approached the new bride, his strong hands tickled feminine arms. Rising to Darcy's neck, his fingernails teased soft skin. Chills tingled Darcy's body. Slipping his fingers through her hair, the stepbrother-husband massaged her scalp. Moving in toward her mouth, his lips kissed hers. Returning his hungry hands to her wedding gown, he yanked the strapless dress downward. Darcy's slip fell with it.

Braless C-cups were revealed. He smiled at her risqué act. Continuing downward, he rode the undulating coaster from thin-waist to wide-hips. However, instead of continuing to her Promised Land, he stopped.

Why's he stopping? Darcy wondered. *He's seen my body plenty of times...is it no longer hot to him? Is he tired of me? I wonder if stepdad's still game...oh stop! I'm sure he wants me and my crazy insecure self!*

Stepbrother Sean calmed Darcy's fears. Lifting her into strong arms, he laid her on the bed diagonally, so her legs hung off the edge. She sank into the oversized feather bed. Her legs spread, revealing white panties with matching garter stockings.

Tossing his stepsister's shoes away, Sean slid his hands up Darcy's legs. Leaving the stockings in-place, he reached for the underwear. Since they were connected to the garter belt, he tore at the soft crotch cloth instead. Darcy gasped at the hunger in her husband's action. She loved the primal desperation in his eyes, craved more edge. The once innocent virgin was becoming a sex-fiend.

The more silk Sean tore, the more tender red flesh was revealed. Darcy's wet pussy lips showed themselves, along with smooth hairless skin. Her sweet scent hit his nose, enticing stepbrother Sean to ravish his new bride.

He started to move in, as Darcy's voice stopped him. "Sean."

"Something wrong?" he asked in worry.

"No...in fact, everything's right."

"Then why stop me?"

"I wanna have your baby."

"Well...I have to *enter* you for that to happen."

"I know...but...I mean like...*now*."

"Tonight? You realize...storks don't deliver babies, right? It takes time to happen."

She tapped his chest with her foot. "Duh! I just don't wanna wait years. I want a part of you...growing inside me."

"Are you even ovulating?"

"I am."

"How do you know?"

"I Googled it."

He felt her forehead, *Slightly warmer than usual*. The rise in body temperature indicated likely ovulation. "Are you sure you don't want to wait? Live out your youth for a while? What if you discover I'm not a good husband? Do you really want to be tied down like that?"

"You'll be a good husband...like you were a good stepbrother. And Sean...trust me...I wanna be tied down...by you," she said seductively, spreading her legs. "Cum inside me."

The mere words made Sean rock hard. His alpha need to breed was activated. He yanked down his pants, too impatient to unbutton them. A 7-inch cock roared out. It was throbbing, begging to mark its territory upon his stepsister's ovulating womb.

Right before he could enter her, Darcy made another request. "And Sean...uh, would you mind..."

"White coat?"

She blushed, "You know me well. I'm kinda embarrassed to say this...but can we pretend I'm prego...at a gyno appointment. You...and the gyno man...screw me in the gyno chair."

Sean paused in thought. *Gyno as in OBGYN? Is the other man my father? Does she mean him...and me...taking her at once? No way. Just stop thinking and fuck for once!* he chastised himself. Sean dug through his luggage, revealing the white doctor coat. Removing his shirt and tie, a muscular body shined in the room light. Slipping the coat on, its open slit revealed tight abs and a thick manly member.

To Darcy's surprise, Sean revealed a stethoscope and latex gloves as well. He snapped the rubbers on his hands, hanging the scope around his neck. Returning to the bedside, he announced, "The doctor is *in*!"

A large smile crossed Darcy's face. "So hot!"

Darcy pushed out her belly, as if fully pregnant. Stepbrother Sean ran his latex hands along the curved ridge, traveling up to exaggerated breasts. "Tie me," she begged.

Sean gazed around frantically, seeking something to tie his stepsister-wife with. *Phone cords!* He thought. He raced for the room's two phones, yanking the cords from both the receiver and wall-jack. Heading back to his willing captive, he tied one wrist to her raised ankle. Then he tied the other wrist to the other raised ankle. Darcy's feet were forced into the air like stirrups.

He pulled her ass cheeks partially off the bed's side. "Let me lube you," he said, dropping to his knees. Burying his face into her sopping red sea, Dr. Abel licked and sucked at his stepsister's slit. Sean spit inside her, letting it drip down her creamy curtains. She was so wet, beads of feminine rain rolled down Sean's face. Drinking every drop, his throat filled with sweet, sticky pleasure.

He felt the redhead's thighs clamp upon his head. The harder she squeezed, the more juice flowed. Air emptied from Sean's lungs, though he refused to quit. As much as he loved her taste as a girlfriend, somehow she tasted even better as a wife. Darcy finally loosened her thigh grip, legs tired from holding the position.

Forcing himself away from her youthful fountain, stepbrother Sean rose. Darcy focused on the 7-inch cock. She begged, "Please knock me up, doctor! I need your cum in me now!"

Lifting Darcy's tied ankles to his shoulders, the alpha step-doctor was determined to do his manly duty. He moved into her soaked slit, placing his cock at her pink palace. Slowly sinking inside her, he changed into his dominating doctor voice. "Mrs. Abel, I'm going to inseminate you now."

"With your penis, doctor?" she played along. "But what about my husband's sperm?"

"He's shooting blanks...so this job calls for a *real* man's seed," he said confidently, sinking deeper into his stepsister.

Darcy gasped, feeling as if fantasy was reality. All 7-inches entered her, Sean's balls touched her ass cheeks. The redhead was so turned on, her tender tunnel expanded well beyond the doc's cock. The idea of a stepbrother seeding her womb drove her wild with taboo lust.

With Darcy's white-stocking feet upon Sean's shoulders, he kissed and licked them. Moving up her foot's veiled sole, he reached the toes. Engulfing each one in his mouth, he sucked all five tiny digits. Needing to touch flesh, he tore the silky fabric away. Feminine feet were unveiled. Sean's tongue bathed every inch of exposed porcelain skin. The tickling feelings trickled through Darcy's body, making her wetter with each attentive lick. It alone was nearly enough to give her an orgasm.

Stepbrother Sean continued pumping his wife the entire time. Once each inch of foot was worshiped, he took the stethoscope's metal disc in latex hand. He placed it upon her heart. The cold steel contrasted heated skin. Her pores rose in stimulation. A pounding drum beat inside Darcy's body and Sean's ears.

Withdrawing from his newlywed wife's pussy, he spit down upon his cock. Placing it against her tight asshole, it would be his first time claiming her anally. Being well aware that his father conquered her ass first, Sean couldn't go there. However, Darcy still used the dilator to prepare for her future husband's arrival.

Wasting no time, Sean's hard cock pushed into her dark chamber door. Moving slowly, yet aggressively, he popped the anal ring. Plunging deeper, he discovered unknown tightness. His cock ached from her anal grip. He kept pushing, arriving balls deep. Darcy did her breathing exercises, accepting stepbrother cock without complaint.

Soft moans escaped her, the first impalement burning and stretching her hole. After a few more anal strokes, she began to relax. The harder he crashed into her ass, the more her belly naturally protruded. Although she admitted her two doctor fantasy, she didn't dare speak of the man in her mind.

"I'll need another doctor to assist me," he announced, granting Darcy's wish. Sean stuffed two latex fingers in his stepsister's pussy. Then a third and fourth were added. Soon, Darcy was fucked

18

in both holes, cock and fingers. Though in her mind, it was her stepfather's cock joining them.

The curvy redhead felt an orgasmic buzz building within her body. Sean suddenly removed his fingers from the soaked snatch. Although she wanted more, her buzz returned as her step-husband removed the scope. In a bold move, he wrapped the cord around his stepsister's soft neck. Shocked, yet not unpleased, Darcy awaited her husband's action. Putting total trust in him, she went limp in submission.

He tightened the chokehold, constricting her throat, restricting air. Her belly heaved further outward the harder he pulled. All the while, he continued banging away inside his wife's tight ass.

Every muscle in the doctor's arms strained, veins swelled to a popping point. Darcy began choking, struggling for air. However, Sean just erotically strangled her harder. To her shock, the more nervous Darcy was, the hotter and wetter she got. By the time all air was denied her, she'd drenched the bed's edge. Her heart pounded even harder, tied hands reached to remove her husband's hold. The actions were to no avail.

Giving up on fighting it, the stepsister submitted to her husband's dominance. Embracing the edgy act, she zoned-in on the incredible tingling buzz. Dizziness encircled her like a ballet of dark angels. She no longer wanted to stop it, craving the alliance of Sean's plunging cock and harsh erotic asphyxiation.

Just as erotic hypoxia set in, Darcy imagined her stepfather again. She could see him choking her while her stepbrother fucked her. Just then, she exploded into orgasm. Unable to make a sound, her body shook in fits. Fireworks burst inside her mind with streams of reds, yellows, and bright whites.

Sean's alpha need to seed grew more desperate. At that point, his mission traveled well beyond pleasure. He withdrew from ass to pussy, aiming his manly weapon into Darcy's chamber. The stepsister's body tensed so tightly, her spasming pussy forced Sean's cum out.

A loud grunt filled the air, as Sean crashed into Darcy. A blast of white life flooded her birth canal. Thick white streams of heavy seed seeped into the cervix, invading the curvy redhead's womb.

All the while, Sean's choking grip squeezed tighter. The two of them just kept cumming, each entranced by thoughts of fertility. Darcy began to blackout, as Sean's last load soaked her. He released his grip, allowing his stepsister to breathe again. A gush of air filled her lungs, as she desperately replenished the life-giving element.

Sean withdrew, untying his wife's wrists and ankles. He tied her thighs shut, trapping her slit like solid-steel doors. He wasn't letting one ounce of sperm escape her. The couple embraced tightly, each of them imagining their future life together.

Darcy drifted to sleep, picturing birthday parties and family vacations. However, she was woken multiple times by an inserted cock. Like primitive man, Sean fucked her whenever and wherever he wanted. Placed in pile driver and doggie-style positions, the redheaded stepsister was constantly filled with stepbrother cum.

As they both finally settled, Sean couldn't fight a fear from within his mind. *What if I can't impregnate her...my father has cases of infertility every day. What if...the scenario we enacted comes true? What if I was the guy shooting blanks? My pride would be destroyed. I couldn't let some other guy's sperm do the job...they could be a serial killer for all I know. What in the hell would I do?*

*****

Tim Abel stared in the bathroom mirror. A five o'clock shadow peppered his face. Such disorder was uncharacteristic of him, as a clean-shaven face represented professionalism, control. It was crucial that he display such strength to patients. Of course, he hadn't had control of his life since losing his wife.

Rinsing the razor blade with blazing hot water, he touched it to his cheek. Feeling the harsh steel sting, he removed it. He imagined slicing a wrist, letting blood spill everywhere. It was a common fantasy, though the spilled blood was never his. It belonged to someone else.

Placing the razor to his cheek again, he gazed into the fogging mirror. Wiping the condensation away with his free hand, a shocking site appeared. "You!" he shouted, seeing the face of the drunk driver replace his own.

He drove his bladed fist into the glass, cracking it in two. A large shard broke off, shattering into the sink. Tim looked up again, hoping beyond all hope his enemy was still there. To his disappointment, only *he* remained.

Dropping the razor, Tim walked away. Something was very wrong. Having imagined hurting the drunk driver in his mind, it was the first time it spilled into reality. Dr. Abel couldn't escape the demon from his past. The truth was…he wasn't sure if he wanted to run away or towards it.

*****

Day turned to night. Tim Abel drove his BMW down a dark, desolate road. He was tired, having tended an overbooked load of patients that day. Though he wasn't headed home. Putting foot to gas, he sped towards the spot of his wife's death.

Knowing its exact location, he retraced her path every night. Her final flip was in the near distance, within eyesight. Suddenly, a bright pair of headlights blazed forward. In the opposite lane, Tim thought nothing of it. However, as the lights got brighter, he realized something.

"Is that car on the wrong side of the road? I think he's coming at me!"

The opposite car raced forward with blazing speed, faster than Dr. Abel could react. Tim jerked the wheel, attempting to avoid a head-on collision. However, the car swerved in his direction. It was clearly aiming for the doctor, hunting him down. Tim shouted in horror. Right before contact, the headlights faded. It was a souped-up Mazda, favored by drag racers.

It was the same exact car that hit his wife, head-on.

Tim gasped in disbelief, freezing in fear. He'd only seen the drunk's vehicle demolished in a junkyard. The doctor remembered seeing it compacted into scrap, regretting never destroying it himself.

However, it was suddenly whole again. The drunk's vehicle rammed into Tim's car, crushing every ounce of metal. Tim felt it smash every bone in his body, just like his wife felt. Though after the excruciating pain, he was denied the right to die, to join his love.

Skidding off road into a ditch, Dr. Abel gazed around. There was no other car in sight, no accident. Stepping out of the vehicle, he was in the exact spot his wife's car landed. He trembled, realizing, *I need help...damn it. I need it now!*

*****

Tim Abel entered a therapist's office. He sat in the cold waiting room, stiff and uncomfortable. Such a setting was not a norm for the man, as giving up control was unthinkable. His motto was, *Doctors don't go to doctors...no matter what type of doctor they are! Physical or mental health...I only trust my own knowledge of medicine. The others are a bunch of quacks.*

However, the darkness, which once burned his photo albums, grew darker. It neared unspeakable acts. He knew if something didn't change soon, he'd act upon them. Though as minutes ticked in the waiting room, fear of the unknown overtook him. *I'll take my chances on my own,* he thought, heading toward the door.

Another door opened, an attractive 40-year-old blond exited. "Mr. Abel?" she asked.

Without a thought, Tim corrected her. *"Doctor...Abel,"* he said, stopping his flight. He turned to see the attractive woman.

Impressed by the man's powerful response, she momentarily felt like the one in a position of submission. That power quickly changed back again. She extended a friendly hand, "I'm Dr. Shelly Cole."

Tim accepted Shelly's greeting. The look of surprise was on his face. He didn't expect to feel a bold grip, matching his own. "Hello," he said coldly and untrusting. "I was under the belief...you were a man."

"What gave you that impression?"

He paused in thought. "I just saw Dr. Cole...not your first name."

"Is that an issue for you? I can refer you to a fellow male colleague...if it makes you more comfortable."

"No...I'm not a misogynist...if that's what you're implying."

"Relax, Dr. Abel...I'd never say such a thing," she assured.

"But you're thinking it," he said in an insulted tone.

"Did you come to discuss my issues...or yours?"

He exhaled, "Sorry."

"No reason to apologize, doctor. You were just speaking your thoughts...something I encourage. Now tell me...why were you leaving? Did you not like my magazine selection?" she asked, smiling.

"I...think this was a mistake."

"We haven't even started yet...how do you know?"

"I just know," he declared.

"Tell me doctor, what if one of your patients walked out before you could treat them? Would they be better off giving in to fear...or worse?"

"I'm not afraid!" he proclaimed.

"Then come inside...give me a chance."

"Fine," he said, puffing his alpha chest. The 54-year-old man strutted toward Dr. Shelly Cole's office.

*****

Shelly shut the door, seeing Tim Abel studying her many diplomas on the wall. "Do I make the credential cut?"

"Just seeing where you went to school...that's all."

"I was just teasing, doctor. Take a seat," she said, studying his nervous body language. Waiting for him to sit on the couch, she followed in her leather chair. "Tell me why you're here today."

He exhaled again, pausing before his response. "Well to start...I'm seeing things."

"What kind of things? Ghosts?"

"I don't believe in ghosts, Dr. Cole. I'm not a nutcase...don't treat me like one."

"I apologize if I offended you, but you have to work with me."

"Fine. It's a man."

"Someone you know? A stranger?"

"Both."

"Can you elaborate a little more?"

"He's a stranger that I know."

"OK. How do you know him? Is he an estranged friend?"

"He's no friend of mine. In fact...he's a mortal enemy."

"So he's caused you past grief."

"Yes."

"Have there been any recent events to trigger such visions?"

"No. I mean...he's always on my mind. And to be honest, dark thoughts always follow him. Though now...they've reached a level of obsession which is unhealthy. No, worse than that...dangerous."

"Dangerous? To whom?"

"Myself...others."

"Elaborate. Who else are they dangerous to?"

He paused again, "I don't feel comfortable saying."

"Fair enough," Dr. Shelly Cole said. "Perhaps in time, when I've earned your trust, you'll feel more comfortable."

"Perhaps," he said, rolling his eyes in disbelief.

"Then lets start with something you're comfortable with. Tell me about your life, your family."

"I'm a doctor...my son, Sean is a doctor, and my daughter, Darcy, just graduated high-school. She's my stepdaughter, to be exact, though she's family to me. They both just got married."

"Congratulations. Do you approve of their choice in spouses?"

Tim paused again. "I do...since they're married to each other."

The therapist was the one pausing next. However, after calculating the facts, she smiled, "Very nice."

"I know...you think they'll have a three-headed child."

Shelly's face cringed, as she thought, *How'd he know I was thinking that?* "Never!" she exclaimed. "It's not like they're related by blood. Besides...I'm not here to judge you, doctor. I'm here to help you...I'm your ally."

"For what I'm paying you...you better be."

She smiled again. He paused, staring deeply at her expression. A glimmer shined in his eyes, one that hadn't shined in years. However, it quickly turned to sadness.

"Is something wrong?" she asked.

"No, why?"

"The expression on your face...it was one of sad reflection."

"My wife...*your* smile...reminded me of my wife's," he said in pain.

"Is that not a good thing?" she asked.

"My wife passed away," he said in heartache.

A look of hurt crossed Shelly Cole's face. It was deeper than sympathy, closer to empathy. "I'm so sorry to hear that," she said, rising from her chair to hug the man. The hug was warm, sincere, and heartfelt.

Slow to return the hug, Tim thought, *Why not?* He returned the offering, placing his arms around her curvy body. Her long blond hair draped over his face. A pheromone struck his nose. She was rose-petal scented like his deceased-wife. It wasn't the only fact to awaken his senses.

It was the care in her touch, rubbing his strong back in support. His hands returned the rub, slowly slipping downward. In near trance, his fingers traced her waist, riding the curves of her hips. He slid downward. Reading her like Braille, Shelly was like a roadmap to his past. She was like his wife.

"Excuse me, doctor...can you remove your hands from my...behind?"

A gasp exited Tim Abel's mouth, as he quickly removed his grasp. "I'm so sorry, you must believe me. I didn't mean to do that...you just felt like...*her*. It's just been so long..."

"It's completely fine, doctor...and normal."

"It is?"

"Yes. Transference. Because I asked you to remember her...your feelings temporarily transfer to me. It passes quickly, nothing to worry about."

He shook his head in agreement, even though he knew better. He'd hugged other women since losing his wife, though none of them caused *that* reaction. "Right."

"Tell me about her."

"Debra Smith...the most beautiful blond hair I've ever seen. Eyes as blue as the ocean. Not the Atlantic. More like the Caribbean. Her body...my God! Curves you could sled on for miles. Her hair smelled like roses, skin too."

Shelly saw the love in the man's eyes, pain equaling it. The tone of his voice was passion, a contrast from the stiff man who arrived there. Shelly found herself lost in his words, his voice. Having seen many patients speak of loss and love, no one had affected her in the same way. The realization spooked her.

"You obviously loved her, do you mind telling me how you lost her?"

Tim's face turned from light to darkness. "It was a dark night, rainy. She was driving home from work, a desolate road. Her last words to me were emailed...*I love you*. I always told her I thought technology was robbing our humanity. I'd give anything to tell her directly, hear her voice...one last time. I didn't get *that* opportunity."

"She got into a car accident?"

Tim's face grew cold, angry. "She was murdered."

Shelly Cole's face turned pale. "I'm so sorry to hear that. Was the killer caught?"

"Oh he was caught alright...a month in jail...and a letter of apology to me."

"I never heard of such a light sentence for murder! Did you write him back?"

"I wrote him...though never sent it. I couldn't find the words. There just weren't enough *fuck you's* I could fit on the page to do my anger justice. He was a drunk driver."

A loud gasp sounded from the therapist's mouth. The unorthodox act was not usual for her. However, chills crossed her skin. Dark memories clouded her own mind. "I...don't know what to say..."

Dr. Abel said, "It's OK. It's been ten years now...yet I still can't adequately explain it. It still feels like yesterday. A 24-year-old punk...beer cans filled the floorboards. He had a fresh 12-pack in the passenger seat, a bottle in his hand. Add to that...the fucker was texting. He hit her head-on...totaled both vehicles. My wife was crushed, dead at the scene. The kid...barely a scratch."

A sick look covered Dr. Shelly Cole's face. Her trembling leg jittered the oak floor. She wanted to share her own pain with him, though knew her job was to help him, not visa-versa. "I don't have the words to heal such a tragedy."

"I didn't expect you to. I guess...I just hoped you'd point me in the direction of sanity...before I lose my mind."

Needing to change the subject, she asked, "In all this time...no romance?"

"Nothing worth keeping."

"Let me guess...no one compares?"

"No one *I've* met."

She nodded. "You mentioned a stepdaughter...I'm assuming that was Darcy's mother."

"It was."

"How's her development been?"

"Great. She's a full C-cup now."

"I meant...mental development, doctor."

"Right. My mind has a direction of its own..."

"You're a man, it's expected. Go on."

"She's grown into an amazing person."

"It's good to see the past hasn't stopped her from love."

"She doesn't know."

"About what?"

"The drunk driver."

"Why not?"

"Why hurt her?" he asked. "As you said...she turned out fine."

"Maybe it's time to tell her the truth. More relevant to our purposes here...maybe it's time you spoke the truth."

"I don't understand."

"You've carried this painful secret around...shouldering all the burden yourself...and you wonder why you can't move on?"

"I do it for my stepdaughter...I do it for Darcy!"

"I wonder about *that*."

"Are you calling me a liar?"

"No, doctor...I'm calling you a survivor. Darcy's not the only one you're protecting."

"Then who else?"

"Yourself," she declared.

He rose in anger, "How dare you suggest that! I'm not a selfish man...in fact, I gave up my fucking life to protect her from the pain."

"You did...you're a kind, great man. I could easily leave it there...but my job is to lay the truth out...no matter how much you don't care to hear it. You feared *dealing* with her pain...as much as *seeing* her in it. No one blames you for that."

"So what are you saying? I should tell her now? Then all my problems just suddenly vanish?"

"You're an educated man, Dr. Abel. You know it's much more complicated than that. However...it'll be a start. It's time to travel the road to recovery."

"I can't do it."

"Why not?"

"She'll hate me...for hiding it."

"You're afraid."

"I told you before entering...I'm not afraid!"

"You are! You fear letting go. You fear feeling better. Most of all, you fear being pain-free. You've worn hurt like a cloak, and you fear what's to come. You fear what will happen when you look around and realize you've wasted half your life alone...chasing ghosts!"

Shock filled him, wondering how the therapist could've known his personal pain so well. However, he reacted in vulnerable anger. "Bullshit!" he shouted, rushing for the exit.

"I'm sorry for my tone, Dr. Abel. I just want you to give yourself a chance at life! It's waiting for you!"

He exited. Shelly exhaled, sad to see him go. Though, she was sad for another reason as well. The therapist's wise advice was something she couldn't follow herself.

CHAPTER TWO

Two Months Later

"I'm so sorry, Sean," Darcy pleaded.

"I'm not blaming you...we don't know who's at fault," Sean said in a stressed voice.

"My mother always said fertile women run in the family. We were made to be knocked-up."

"So it's *you* putting the blame on *me*! You think I'm not man enough...that I'm shooting blanks?"

"No, that's not what I mean...well, kinda...but not in a bad way."

"Then you're insulting my manhood in a...*good way?*"

"Not at all, baby. I just don't know what to do. It's been two months, and nothing's happened. Can we see someone?" she asked timidly, knowing Sean hated other doctors.

"No!" he exclaimed.

"But why not?"

"We'll just keep trying until it happens."

"I don't wanna be one of those sad couples...waiting forever to get pregnant. I don't wanna see all my friends pushing babies in strollers, on swings, wishing I was them."

Sean exhaled in stress. "I know, I know. I just...don't want to..."

"Don't want to what? What are you afraid of, Sean?"

"I don't fear anything!"

"You're just like stepdad! Why can't men just admit when they're scared?"

"Fine, you wanna know what scares the living shit out of me? Watching my manhood die before my eyes! That's what scares me, Darcy!"

Darcy put her arms around him. "You're still *my* man, no matter what! Am I any less of a woman if it's my fault?"

"The expectations are different for men. You just don't understand. It's my job to impregnate you, my job to produce offspring. The need's as old as cavemen themselves!"

"Who cares what anyone thinks? Just like our relationship...we didn't get anyone's permission. We did it *our* way."

"I care what *I* think...and it would make *me* a failure. Besides, I don't trust any of these wackos with the results. Half of these OBGYN's are high on narcotics."

Nervousness filled Darcy, fearful to make her suggestion. However, she thought, *What do I have to lose at this point? Screw it, just say it!* "Well...there's always *stepdad*," she said, cringing.

"You can't be serious," Sean accused.

"Just think about it...he's already seen me...*naked*," she looked down, averting her eyes from her stepbrother husband. "And he's so smart! You know you can trust what he says."

Sean knew Darcy was correct. He admired his OBGYN father's knowledge, though he couldn't imagine the man intimately examining Darcy again. However, he also wanted to make her happy. Few things were more important than the alpha-doctor's pride, though his step-wife's joy was one of them. "For you...I'll do it."

Tears entered Darcy's eyes. She kissed his lips. "Thank you, baby. I promise, no matter how it goes, I'll love you until the day I die. You'll always be my man, always!"

He nodded, fear still gleaming in his eyes. Although he didn't say it, his pained inner-thoughts spoke louder than words. *I just hope I can live with the results.*

*****

"Welcome," Tim Abel greeted, entering his exam room.

Darcy was in her medical gown, sitting nervously in the gyno chair. *Me and my big mouthed stupid ideas! Stepdad examining me for infertility while stepbrother husband watches! What was I thinking? Sean will end up killing his own father over jealousy!*

Sean Abel was uncomfortable, never-before entering the family medical practice as a patient. Taking one gaze at the gyno chair, his skin crawled. Seeing the look on his son's face, Tim Abel reached into a drawer, removing a white coat from within. Handing the spare to Sean, he said, "Take the edge off, doctor."

Sean nodded, "Thanks," he said, putting it on. He still felt strange, though like a frightened child with his favorite blanket, it brought a sense of comfort. Unfortunately, *that* security soon faded.

Dr. Tim Abel handed his son a plastic cup. "Go into the bathroom and ejaculate into the sterile cup. We have visual stimulation...magazines...videos...if needed..."

"I know, dad...I work here too."

"I'm just being official," Tim informed his son.

Sean grabbed the cup in humiliation. He headed into the sample room, as Tim approached Darcy in the gyno chair. Both of them looked awkward, remembering the last time they were in the exam room. Orally and anally stimulated by her step-doctor, the redhead felt like she was living it again. As much as she wanted to deny it, the situation turned her on.

Dr. Tim Abel ordered the curvy patient, "Place your feet in the stirrups." Darcy complied, exposing her wet snatch. After snapping on latex gloves, Tim stepped between his stepdaughter's spread legs.

His mouth watered from the scent of her arousal. The sight of her pink pussy made him rock-hard. Although he no longer had romantic love for Darcy, he couldn't deny the physical pleasure he got from anally conquering her.

"Before I start, I need to ask you a few questions. Sean too."

"Can I take my legs down, cover up during it?"

"No," he said, failing to give a reason.

"OK, doctor...stepdad," she said submissively.

The door opened, as a white-coated Sean slowly walked out. He was red from both strain and embarrassment. "Here," he said, holding the cum-filled cup in his hands. Unable to look his father in the eye, he stared downward.

Unhindered by such situations, the senior doctor took the cup without pause. Pulling out a black marker, he wrote the name Abel on it, putting it aside. Darcy focused on the cup, thinking, *Wow, that's one big load. Could he actually be turned on by this...or was it the porn mags? Probably the porn.*

"Take a seat, Sean."

"I'd rather stand," he said, not wanting to feel like a patient.

"No problem," Tim responded. "First, I want to say...in most cases, we prefer to wait 12 months to officially diagnose infertility. Are you sure you don't want to wait and see if it happens naturally?"

"No," Darcy chimed in. "I want it now."

"OK, onto the first question. *Family history.* Well...no need for that." Tim checked the box. "Did your last partner, predating your spouse, have any type of sexually transmitted diseases? Actually, lets skip that one as well." Knowing that Darcy's last partner was the doctor himself, they all appreciated the omission. "In fact...let's just move on to the examination," Tim said.

"Good idea," Sean agreed.

"Can I go pee now? You told me to drink all this water...I think I'm gonna burst."

"We'll get to that soon enough, Darcy," the step-doctor assured.

Stepping in-between the redheaded patient's legs, his hunger for her grew. Sean quickly joined him, both men crowded for a spot. Darcy's heart thumped hard. She stared at her stepfather and stepbrother lodged between her spread thighs.

Dr. Tim Abel announced, "I'm going to perform a series of tests. Since the man's responsible for 30% of infertility cases, women 70%, Darcy's tests will be a bit more...invasive. We'll start with a transvaginal ultrasound."

"This probably won't work on me...since I'm not a transvestite. Can we just move on to the next test?" Darcy asked.

"Nice try," Tim responded.

"Ultra...*sound*...so you'll be looking in my ears, right? Testing my hearing?" Darcy asked in hope, even though she knew better.

"Wrong end," Tim announced. "This *sound...*is in your vagina. Sound waves, of course."

Dr. Tim Abel unveiled a thick 4-inch probe. It was attached by wire to a computer monitor. Thicker than the usual transvaginal probe, it stimulated the patient to get more accurate results. He added a disposable sheath over the plastic wand.

The doctor activated the monitor screen. He added ultrasound gel to the probe's end, spreading Darcy with latex fingers. Then he slowly slid it into her moist mound. She moaned, legs stiffened, feet dug into steel stirrups. The probe went from thinner to widest at the base. With every inch, Darcy was stretched open further

It seemed unending, pressing her full bladder from the inside. Multiple sensations struck her, ranging from a urination sting to pained insertion to sexual heat. She couldn't figure out which one would win out. She silently thought, *I will not cum! It was bad enough doing that in front of each step-doctor separately! I can only imagine how embarrassing it would be together! Uh!*

The feeling only got worse as Dr. Tim Abel pressed upward on the probe. Feeling her G-spot squashed, Darcy imagined herself leaping from the gyno chair, head stuck in ceiling. Orgasm was creeping closer, her fluids spilling like nectar of the gods.

Dr. Tim Abel activated the probe. Sound waves sailed through Darcy's vaginal velvet, a black and white image appeared on the monitor. The ovaries and uterus were on screen. Tim moved it around fast and roughly, up and down, side to side. "Oh-ly crapola!" she shouted, tensing hard.

"Try not to tense," Stepfather Abel instructed.

Not hearing a word he said, Darcy's kegel muscles contracted. Choking the slick and slippery wand with her pussy, her sexual nerves were ablaze with fire. Each probing struck a different part of her. The most painfully stimulating was the G-spot gland. Trying to hold her urine in, Darcy's tightening canal burned with greater sexual flames.

While the two step-doctors watched the monitor screen, sweat beaded down Darcy's forehead. Her breath huffed, heart raced. The curvy redhead bit her bottom lip to a bleeding point. Grasping the chair rails, she silently begged herself, *Don't cum...please...don't do it!*

The slick probe sailed back, forth, up, down, left, right. "I'm cumming!" Darcy shouted, shocking the two doctors. They looked over, watching the redhead shake like a runaway washing machine. Her eyes rolled upward, teeth gnashed as one. Tim Abel kept the probe going, knowing better than to leave a patient aimlessly grinding.

Darcy's feet slipped from the stirrups, shutting her thighs, smashing the wand between them. She humiliatingly humped the thick invader, cumming upon the medical instrument. Pained pleasure reverberated through her curvy body, coating the plastic covering in feminine cream.

As she calmed, her worst fear was realized. *OMG! I orgasmed in front of my stepfather and stepbrother together. Husband or not...this was so embarrassing! Ooohhh...I really gotta pee!* "Can I go now? Like...as in...pee?"

"Absolutely," Dr. Tim Abel said.

Darcy quickly attempted to escape, Dr. Tim Abel stopped her from exiting. "Stay seated."

"Don't I get to use the porn bathroom too?" Darcy asked.

"No. I need to perform a luteinizing hormone test, checking to see if you're ovulating properly. I'll need two separate fresh, sterile samples. I'll switch containers mid-stream," he said to both his son and stepdaughter's shock. Sean never took samples like that. Taking the cup in hand, Tim pressed on Darcy's abdomen. Locating the bladder, he pressed hard, forcing the curvy redhead to urinate.

Darcy's face turned fire red. Her body tightened and tensed. She already had to pee before arriving, though the latex press made it intensely worse. The more Darcy fought it, the more pressure her stepfather applied. Slight moans sounded from the curvy redhead.

Gazing over at her stepbrother husband, Darcy hoped he'd step in. He did exactly that. To her surprise, it wasn't to stop it, but join in. Sean thought, *If I can't beat him, I'll join him damn it!* Slapping on a pair of latex gloves, both of Sean Abel's hands pressed upon his stepsister wife's bladder.

Tim proudly smiled, happy to work in tandem with his son. In their time working together, it was a first. Suddenly, Darcy's loud gasp filled the room. Leaving Sean to press, Dr. Tim Abel grabbed two specimen cups. He held a plastic cup in each hand, placing one at the base of his stepdaughter's ass. After more intense pressing, Darcy's hard fought battle for urination was finally lost. She was forced to let go, letting a stream sail from her inner depths.

One step-doctor kept pressure on her abdomen, keeping his wife flowing, the other spread her wide, collecting her offering. Darcy froze in forced submission. *I'm peeing in front of my stepfather and stepbrother...holy hell...someone shoot me now!*

With no other option, she kept filling the specimen cup. The longer it took to empty her bladder, the more humiliated she became. Though her stiffened nipples told a different story. As much as she didn't want to admit it, the voyeuristic show turned her on. Being watched by the two step-doctors simultaneously, aroused her beyond words.

In mid-stream, Tim switched cups. "Just keep going, don't stop," he instructed.

As the last trickle landed, Dr. Tim Abel capped and labeled both specimen cups. Sean Abel wiped Darcy with a disinfectant pad, making his step-sister wife sting with pleasure.

Both step-doctors remained between Darcy's thighs. Tim lubed his co-doctor's finger with a squirt. The surprised 30-year-old gladly accepted. "We'll perform a duel digital exam," Tim said proudly.

"You want my...assistance? Really, dad?"

"I'd be honored to have your help, son."

Darcy's mouth dropped open. *Are they really gonna finger me...together? Oh shit...this is nuts...and hot! And dangerous! Could I cum again? I've had multiples before. Shit!*

The two men entered their fingers into the sopping pink slit. Each one pushed forward, slowly. Tim examined one silky side, Sean the other. Stepfather and stepbrother sank deeper into Darcy's creamy cavern. Reaching their latex knuckles, they spun their fingers in circles.

They stretched their curvy young patient wide. Each one touched her G-spot, pressing upward, making Darcy squirm more. The deeper they moved inside her, the hotter each sexual nerve fired up. Wetness trickled from her pussy; orgasm wasn't far behind it.

Both men removed their fingers from the juicy fruit. They touched their index fingers to thumb, pulling sticky fluid apart. A cloudy string appeared. "Looks normal to me," Sean said.

"A normal sign of arousal," Tim said, making both Darcy and Sean blush.

Next, the doctor revealed a speculum. Spreading his stepdaughter wide, he slipped it inside her pink paradise. Clicking the metal medical tool, he stretched Darcy open. More evidence of a whitish wonderland showed itself, cloudy streams of quim awaited.

Grabbing a bristle brush, Dr. Tim Abel swabbed the vaginal cells in swirls. Darcy squirmed, though didn't cum again. However, the most involved exam had yet to begin. For the last act, the senior doctor grabbed a thin, flexible tube with a small, lighted camera on its end. Between the prior lubing and Darcy's natural wetness, he didn't need another.

The doctor attached the medical contraption to the monitor, activating it again. Not knowing what to expect, the curvy redhead tensed in nervousness. Still spread by the speculum, she couldn't stop the tube from entering her slippery slit.

Darcy was fine until it hit her cervical ring. She squirmed, reaching downward to pull it out. Tim ordered, "Hold her down, Sean!"

The strong stepbrother pinned his stepsister down, exposing her breasts in the struggle. Darcy removed her legs from the stirrups, kicking at her stepfather doctor, trying to stop him from entering her womb.

With no other choice, Tim Abel went for plan B. Having dealt with manically panicking patients before, a sleepy injection was the answer. The senior doctor readied an IV. "Tape her hand to the chair, we need to keep her steady for the needle!" Stepfather Tim ordered his son.

As bad as he felt, Sean knew it was for his wife's own good. Grabbing the medical tape, he secured his stepsister's arms to the handrails, wrists up.

"Sean...don't do this. I don't want a shot!" Darcy begged.

"Relax, baby...it's just twilight," he said, swabbing her soft skin at the inner elbow area. "You'll feel it less...fight it less."

Darcy's stepfather administered the needle, watching his mostly nude, curvy stepdaughter squirm more. He opened the IV, letting the liquid sedative flow. The fight calmed, her body capitulated to her step-doctors. Darcy's eyes got heavy, stepbrother's gloved fingers slipped through red hair, comforting her into a heavy daze.

The patient went limp in the gyno chair. Dr. Tim Abel placed Darcy's feet back in the stirrups. Sean taped them into place, spreading his unconscious stepsister wide. Tim guided the tube deeper inside, threading the exploratory camera through the cervical ring. Looking at the monitor's screen, Dr. Abel snaked the camera throughout her womb. He examined each ovary closely, ensuring their full health.

In the midst of his exam, his son further exposed Darcy's breasts. Sean groped them roughly. Seeing his father's stare, Sean said, "I figured...a breast exam couldn't hurt."

Tim nodded, "Good idea. In fact..." Tim said, placing his finger against Darcy's asshole, he pressed inward to the sleepy sphincter. "I think a rectal exam is in order as well."

Darcy gently moaned, feeling multiple sensations fill her. It felt like a dream, like her fantasy, being examined by her stepfather and stepbrother simultaneously. Tim Abel pushed deeper into her womanhood, exploring every inch. He also swirled his finger inside her anal wonderland, checking her rectum.

Pressing a button, Dr. Tim Abel released a biopsy needle from the inner tube. A tissue sample was collected from the uterus. Pleasure and pain buzzed Darcy's hazy mind. Her body ached to cum again, fighting sleep itself to do so. She could feel her stepbrother pinching her nipples, roughly squeezing her breasts. At the same moment, she felt her stepfather's tools invade her ass and pussy. However, she could only enjoy it in theory, as exhaustion captured her.

Though Darcy couldn't fully appreciate the moment, Sean Abel did. As much as it made him jealous, watching his stepfather command his wife brought unexpected comfort. *I trust my father to do what's right...for the both of us. She's in good hands...and I have no doubt that by the end of this...she'll be pregnant.*

*****

"Mr. Abel?" Dr. Shelly Cole asked in shock. She was headed home for the night.

"Miss Cole...I mean, Dr. Cole, I'm sorry to surprise you like this...I know I don't have an appointment. I see you're leaving...I'll come back another time," he said, quickly turning for the exit.

"Doctor...stop," she demanded.

Tim Abel was not used to orders, yet he obeyed. Turning back to face her, he awaited her words.

"Come inside, please."

*****

Inside the office, the doctor was as uncomfortable as their first meeting, two months ago. He sat on the couch, wanting to run out.

Shelly Cole sat in her seat. "It's good to see you again, doctor."

"And you," he said in a stiff tone.

"It's been a while."

"It has."

"The last time we spoke, you mentioned a stepdaughter...Darcy, I believe," she said.

Tim's phone suddenly rang. It was a song called, *La Vie en Rose*, by Louis Armstrong. "Speaking of my stepdaughter...that's her ringtone. I'll call her back. And yes, she introduced me to ringtones. All this phone technology's foreign to me."

"Great song."

"Yeah, I call her my red rose...the song was fitting. You have a good memory...after all these months...and just one meeting."

"It's easy to remember when you care about people," she said sincerely. "I thought about you often these last two months. I was worried about you."

"Why me?"

She blushed, realizing she'd been too honest. "Uh...I worry about all my patients' well-being. But more specific to your case...my worry stemmed from your inner-anger...deeply harbored pain."

"Ah, so it's *myself* I need saving from. I'm beginning to recall why I ran out of here...haven't returned."

Dr. Cole smiled warmly, "Most of us are our own worst enemies, doctor."

"You included?"

Now Shelly Cole was the one to pause. She appeared apprehensive. "I'll play along. Sure, some times of my life...worse than others."

"Not nearly as dark as my situation."

"You shouldn't *assume*...as the saying goes...it makes an ass out of you and...well, *just* you. I'm sorry, that was unprofessional..."

"No, you're correct. How would I know your pain? Unless you're willing to tell me..."

"Doctor, this is your treatment, not mine."

"Right, sorry again. None of my business."

"It's fine...let's get back to you," she said, wearing an uncomfortable expression.

Tim Abel shifted in his chair, wishing Shelly Cole had taken the spotlight instead. Though more than that, he wanted to know about her. The look in her eyes was strangely familiar to him. He'd suddenly realized, it was the same pain which stared back in the mirror. "Go ahead, ask what you want to ask."

"Before I do...promise me something," she requested.

"Sure."

"Give me a chance. Don't run out on me...disappearing for two months. Don't quit before you've even begun. Allow me to help you, doctor...please, sir."

Tim Abel nodded. "You have my word."

"Thank you. We'll get back to Darcy in a moment...but first, I'd like to discuss the visions from last session."

"Wow, you *really* have a good memory. I still see him...more often with each day. I see the drunk driver so much...he's become normal to me."

"The dark thoughts still there?"

"Darker than ever."

"Are you ready to talk about it...tell me what those thoughts are?"

He exhaled, stress plastered his face. "I am."

"Were they thoughts of self-harm?"

"At one point, yes. Though, those days have long passed."

"Thoughts of harming others?"

Dr. Abel turned pale, gulping. *Should I dare tell her? She can have me arrested...doctor-patient confidentiality is easily broken. Though it's that look in her eyes...it's like, she knows...feels my pain. I think I can trust her...I think I can take the risk.* The look on his face answered for him. "Just one."

Strangely, Shelly Cole didn't look surprised. "You don't have to tell me who...but can you please tell me why?"

"Mike Robertson."

"Who is he to you?"

"A name I'll never forget. A man...no, he's not a man. The scum I'll curse until the day I die. He's the devil of my world."

"Explain."

"He murdered my wife!" Tim Abel shouted angrily.

"I'm sorry, doctor. I know how hard it is to speak his name. Though, is harming him the answer?"

"Aren't you supposed to tell me that?"

She paused, as if she was hoping to hear it herself. Then, she remembered to recite the responsible thing. "Of course, it's always wrong to harm anyone..."

"No, it's wrong to harm the *innocent*. It's wrong to get behind the wheel of a *car*...to drive into someone head-on! It's NOT wrong to take an axe to that scumbag's head...to burn him alive. Or eye for an eye...drive him right into a brick wall!" he shouted at the top of his lungs. The normally composed man was beet red, trembling. He nearly foamed at the mouth with rabidity.

Shelly's heart pounded, fist clenched. She wanted nothing more than to scream, *Do it! Do it now...for me!* Of course, she took an oath against such advice. "Relax, doctor! I shouldn't have to school you in the dangers of raised blood pressure! You'll be the one to die, if you don't take a breath!"

Hearing her words, the doctor sat back down. He grasped his salt and pepper hair in frustration. Wheeling her chair closer to Tim, Shelly placed her hand on his knee. Her mere touch calmed the doctor like only one other had: his deceased wife.

"Your kids...think about them. They don't want to lose their father...have him sent to jail."

"I don't plan on going to jail."

"Such a crime leaves evidence behind...things you can't anticipate, clues to your identity you'll never realize exist!"

"Good point," Tim said, thinking, *It almost sounds like she's considered killing before.* After taking another look at her feminine curvy frame, he thought, *Not a chance.*

"Let's not speak of such pain...let's talk about good things. Darcy. Tell me about her."

"She's an amazing girl. Just turned 19."

"You really care for her. I see it in your eyes."

"I do. When she lost her mother...she became my world. I wanted to save her, protect her..."

"And you did that."

"I tried."

"It sounds like you did a fine job of raising her."

"I wasn't perfect."

"No one is."

"No...I did a terrible thing. In giving everything to protect her, I abandoned my son in the process."

"I'm sure he forgives you."

"He does...though it's myself I can't forgive."

"And this brings us back to my point...the one I made two months ago. Doctor, your son wasn't the only one you abandoned that day. You abandoned yourself as well...abandoned life itself."

Another deep exhale exited Tim Abel's mouth. It was like he finally capitulated his denial. He was too exhausted to fight anymore. "You're right."

"It's time to lift your burden. It's time to tell Darcy the truth. She deserves to know how her mother died, and you deserve to release this secret you've carried around all these years. I know you think avoiding truth helped you both...but it hasn't."

"She'll never forgive me for lying."

"You didn't lie...you just didn't tell. If Darcy's the loving girl you describe, she'll understand...I promise."

After a long pause, a look of resolution crossed Tim Abel's face. "Can that really free all the pain?"

"I don't know, doctor. Every person processes pain and release different. But I do know it's worth the shot."

"OK, Dr. Cole. For you...I'll do it."

"No, Dr. Abel. Do this for you. It's time to start healing."

CHAPTER THREE

"Welcome back," Dr. Tim Abel greeted his son and stepdaughter.

They flashed nervous smiles at him, unsure of what was to come. The prior appointment was interesting to say the least. "Hi, stepdad," Darcy said. "I think I'm ovulating...as you asked."

"Great...I'll just check to make sure. It's important for today's exam."

"Father," Sean Abel said, nodding hello. "Can you loan me a medical coat again?"

"I don't believe you'll need it, son."

"Why's that?" Sean asked suspiciously.

"Because this particular exam doesn't require clothes."

"For Darcy," Sean stated.

"For both," Dr. Tim Abel informed.

Both their faces turned to shock. Darcy said, "Umm...total nakedness?"

"Yes," Tim declared.

"Dad, I'm a doctor. There's no exam I know of requiring a couple to be naked."

"Correct, son. A General Practitioner wouldn't be familiar with it, but an OBGYN would."

"Don't forget the T, step-dad."

Sean looked at her with a crazy gaze. "T?"

"OBGYN and T...for throat," she said.

Sean looked at his stepfather in an even more confused manner. Dr. Tim Abel said, "It's a specialty I studied in my spare time. Never mind that...we must solve this infertility problem! The exam is called a post coital test."

"Wait a minute! Post as in *after*...coital as in *sex*?" Sean asked in disbelief.

"Relax, son. I won't be present during the act."

"Since when is sex sanctioned in a medical setting?" Sean questioned.

"It's often not...the couple usually returns home for a few hours. Unfortunately, they often return too late. The results get skewed. I won't risk that with my son and stepdaughter. You have my word. By the end of our time together...Darcy will carry the Abel seed...no matter what I have to do to achieve it."

"So we'll get it on...in here?" Darcy asked.

"I'll move you to one of the more comfortable rooms. One with a plush medical table."

"Tell me what happens...*post*...sex," Sean demanded.

"I'll examine Darcy...test the sperms survival rate time. Plus check the acidity of her cervical mucus. It's a very important test to administer."

The couple's hearts pounded in unison, as they knew it had to be done. They nodded, both remaining silent.

*****

Entering the room, Dr. Tim Abel walked them in. Sean exhaled, thinking, *I've had sex in here before...though as a doctor. There's something about being a patient that sickens me. It's like my power's been stripped away, like I've been neutered! Instead of feeling horny, I feel nauseous. This isn't a good start. Can I even get it up? Shit, why'd I even think that? The thought alone will cause it!*

Tim entered, handing Sean a white medical coat. "Your requested coat," Tim said.

The 30-year-old doctor paused, staring at it. He set it aside. "At the moment, I just don't feel very doctor-like," Sean said.

Dr. Tim Abel nodded, approaching Darcy. He revealed a long thermometer. "I'll need you to remove your pants and underwear, Mrs. Abel," Tim said in his professional voice.

"I thought you were leaving us alone in here?" Sean asked in a stressed voice.

"This is just to assure ovulation," Tim said. "As you know...a rise in body temperature is always a sign of it."

Darcy exhaled deeply, obeying her stepfather. Removing her shoes and socks, her cute feet were unveiled. She unbuttoned her jeans, dropping them to her ankles, kicking them away. Pausing with hands on her white panties, she stared up at her entranced stepfather and stepbrother. While Sean had a stressed gaze upon him, Tim Abel was visibly hard with lust.

The redhead pulled down her underwear. Her red pubic hair had grown back since her last shaving. Sean wanted to see the flaming beauty contrast against her pale pussy again.

Having not seen such a site, Darcy's stepfather got even more erect. "I need you to lie on the table," he said, patting the paper-lined surface. She approached him, as he lifted her up to the flat bed. Lying flat, her heart beat faster. "Spread your legs," her stepfather ordered.

Obeying the step-doctor, her thighs parted. She could feel her stepbrother's eyes burning, seething with jealousy. However, her thoughts were quickly removed from him. Tim Abel spread the wet, pink lips further apart. Darcy gasped, feeling the cold glass thermometer enter her.

It sank deeper, nearly swallowed by her creamy canal. Stepfather Tim shut Darcy's legs, locking the probe tightly inside her. She wiggled, feeling the glass poke at her cervix. Tim Abel kept his latex hand on her soft thigh, arousing the curvy redhead. Gazing at her stepbrother, she saw his discomfort grow.

The longer it stayed inside her, the wetter she got. Darcy's thighs were spread again, the thermometer removed. Her humiliation rose as her stepfather grabbed a rag, saying, "There's sexual discharge blocking the gauge...I'll just clean it off..."

"That happens a lot, right stepdad?" Darcy asked.

"Not really," Tim Abel said, making the couple cringe in further embarrassment.

"99.6. You're correct...ovulation is occurring," Tim confirmed. "I'll leave you two love birds to enjoy each other. Take your time...no rush."

Tim Abel exited the room, as Darcy and Sean stared at each other. "Let's get this over with," Sean said, having no intentions of making love. He kicked off his shoes and socks, dropped his slacks and boxers in one shot. Like Darcy, he left his shirt on. He stroked his flaccid cock, trying to quickly get a rise. It wasn't cooperating.

"Maybe this will help," Darcy said, removing her shirt. Her bra came off, revealing perky C-cups. Sean's curvy stepsister-wife lie naked on the medical table. The muscular doctor felt his cock rise again. Darcy asked, "The doctor coat? For old time's sake," she winked.

He flung off his shirt, revealing a muscular body. After putting on the coat, he quickly leapt up on the medical table, knowing his erection might not last long. As he placed his cock head to Darcy's slit, he heard his head nurse's voice outside the door. Then he heard his father talking, "They're trying to conceive. Who knows, it may even be happening as we speak."

All the pressure and shame struck Dr. Sean Abel again. His mind returned to the submissive patient, at the mercy of his own father. Right before he could penetrate her, he went soft again. "Fuck!" he shouted.

"It's OK, baby," Darcy said, kissing him. "It's cold in here...it's like when we had sex in the pool, you shrank."

"This is different...I just...can't do it."

"What can we do? We need this...for a baby," she said sadly.

Stepping down from the table, Sean put on his pants. Leaving his white coat on, a muscular chest peeked out the slit. He exited the room, joining his father and blond head nurse. His sexy feminine colleague let out an impressed gasp, having never seen her boss so exposed. She quickly turned away in bashfulness.

"Dad...we need to talk," Sean said stiffly.

"Sure," Tim Abel said, joining his son. The head nurse walked away.

Sean whispered, "I...can't...*you know*."

"Ejaculate?"

"The cow before the milk," Sean cryptically hinted.

"You can't get erect?" Tim asked loudly.

A collective gasp sounded from everyone around. The staffs' gazes turned in Sean's direction.

"Shhhh! Dad, my employees just heard you say that! They'll never respect an impotent boss!"

"Oh don't be ridiculous...you hold their paychecks in your hands...they'll bow down in reverence. I can solve your problem."

"Viagra?"

"No, that chemical garbage alters your sperm."

"Then what?"

Dr. Tim Abel turned to Sean's head nurse. "Mia."

"Yes, doctor?" she asked.

"Your assistance is needed."

Oh shit! Sean thought silently. By the time he could protest, she was standing before both bosses. Tim Abel whispered quietly in her ear. She blushed ten shades deeper. "Yes, doctor," she said. Following instructions, she immediately went into the exam room.

"What did you tell her?" Sean asked.

"To help out."

"How?"

"Don't worry...it's an old-fashioned remedy. Works like a charm. It was standard practice when I started out. Just get in there and seed your stepsister...or wife."

Stressed beyond words, Sean let out another exhale. "Fuck it," he said, entering the room, slamming the door behind him.

Darcy was uncomfortable with the new female guest. "What's happening, Sean?" she asked.

"This is my head nurse, Darcy. Don't worry, she's just going to help...somehow."

Unable to look Sean in the eyes, head nurse Mia snapped on a pair of latex gloves. Doctor, please remove your pants."

Still unsure what was happening, Sean just wanted to get it over with. Removing his pants, his still flaccid cock appeared. He blushed as much as the nurse did, humiliated that his employee was seeing him exposed, far from his glory.

She bent down in front of him, grasping his cock with her latex palm. "First, I'm going to perform a milking of the penis," she said.

Darcy gasped, having never seen her step-husband touched by another woman. Sean tensed, feeling his sexy blond nurse stroking his manhood. With each masturbating motion, the strong doctor began to grow. He looked up at his curvy redheaded stepsister. Her nipples were swollen and pointed toward the heavens. The scent of her feminine arousal filled the room. Shame masked Darcy's face for feeling such pleasure.

Before he knew it, Sean Abel's cock reached its 7-inch max. His veins swelled, cock throbbed. Head nurse Mia could already see a clear glob of precum seeping from the man-slit. "I think I'm there," he announced. "You can stop now."

"Right...sorry," Mia said in disappointment, releasing her cock-hold. "Please lie on top of your wife...assume missionary position."

OK, I feel like I'm in science class! So mechanical! This sucks! Darcy thought.

Keeping his white coat on, the muscular doctor mounted his stepsister. He positioned himself between her legs. Placing his cock at Darcy's dripping snatch, he awaited his head nurse's action. He began shrinking again, informing the nurse, "My problem is *staying* hard...oh damn that's cold..." he shouted, feeling an unexpected glob of lube part his muscular ass cheeks.

The blond nurse's latex finger touched Sean's asshole, "I need you to bear down, boss," she said.

"Why?" he asked.

"I'm going to massage your prostate to keep you erect," she said, pushing hard into his tight sphincter.

Sean grunted, his strong body pressed into Darcy. The intense feeling made his cock even harder. He plunged into his wife. His newly stiffened spear disappeared into his stepsister's wet wonderland.

Darcy moaned loudly, penetrated without warning. Sean's cock invasion was quick and hard, stretching the pussy lips, snuggling inside velvet blankets. Her strong husband weighed down upon her, sweat rained.

The head nurse went knuckle deep, pressing downward on Sean's prostate. His bottom-up position allowed maximum pressure on the gland. Although the 30-year-old doctor had a prostate exam before, it was never in a sexual situation, nor by an attractive subordinate. With each new wiggling of the latex finger, Sean's cock grew longer, girth wider.

The curvy redhead moaned, feeling her husband bucking like a mad bull. A surge of sexual stamina filled Sean's body. His white coat draped them both, flying through the air like a cape. He pounded his stepsister-wife harder, crashing into her sopping wet pussy. Spits of sweet juice speckled his balls and thighs.

All the while, the blond nurse stimulated the swollen gland within. Placing a second finger at his asshole, she entered another. Sean grunted like a sexually enraged beast, crashing into Darcy like a runaway truck. The feeling was painful enough to make a man cry, pleasurable enough to make him beg.

Their sexy nurse stretched Sean's asshole, plunging into the sexual gland. Every nerve heated, the doctor's ass felt like it was on fire. Thick streams of clear fluid crept through his stiff shaft, spilling into Darcy.

The distinct heavy swell of sperm began its forward march. As humiliating as it was, neither Darcy nor Sean dared stop it.

Watching another woman manipulate her husband drove Darcy wild with jealous lust.

Sean continued pounding his stepsister, every muscle strained to a bulge. Thick arms stretched the medical coat, his tight ass connected to strong thighs and bulbous calves.

The blond nurse's fingers sank deeper inside her boss' ass. She pressed so hard Sean's prostate flattened. Beads of sweat poured from him, baptizing his stepsister in an erotic tempest. He crashed into Darcy so hard she shook with each landing.

Darcy thought, *Don't cum...this isn't for enjoyment! Oh shit, the more I tell myself not to...the more I wanna...CUM!* A high-pitched squeal filled the room, sailing through the whole building. Darcy's curvy body trembled in fits of hot passion. She'd never been fucked so aggressively. Her fire red hair dangled off the table, swaying like flickering flames.

Her stepbrother's cock was so deep it nearly broke through to her womb. She anxiously awaited his cum, hoping seed would finally take hold. Darcy's body tensed, toes grasped, feet spun around in crazed circles. Each of Sean's new thrusts got quicker, his strong chest chaffed his stepsister's stiff nipples.

Feeling Darcy's tender flesh choke his cock, he unleashed seed inside his stepsister. His shout was wolf-like, grainy, gristled and growly. Right as he came, the blond nurse pressed the hardest of all. A tidal wave flooded Darcy's pussy.

With each new spurt of semen, the blond milked his prostate harder. Just when he thought he couldn't fire another round, a new load was forced from inner depths. He just kept cumming, losing control of bodily functions. Shaking with sexual convulsions, he was hostage to latex fingers. He could've kept going all day, though was finally offered mercy as the head nurse withdrew from Sean's ass.

The doctor collapsed on his redheaded wife. The two sat there, reality suddenly taking hold again. As embarrassing as it all was, a greater thought overtook their minds.

Will we ever have a child...or was all this for nothing?

*****

"From the sound of things...I'd say it went well in there," Dr. Tim Abel said, returning to his exam room. Darcy nodded, waiting inside the gyno chair. She wore a gown, feet pressed into the stirrups. Sean was dressed, opting to keep the white coat on. He stood beside his stepsister-wife, looking down in embarrassment.

Tim Abel stepped between his stepdaughter's spread legs. To his disappointment, a large puddle of semen pooled on the chair, flooding the bottom of Darcy's ass cheeks. Snapping on a fresh pair of latex gloves, he entered the speculum inside the curvy redhead.

Already slick with shared love juice, he slid the metal beak contraption inside his patient. Clicking the lever, he forced Darcy's pink pussy open. She gasped with every further inch of gape. Once she was as wide as she'd go, Tim activated an internal speculum light.

Turning to his son, Dr. Tim Abel asked, "Would you like to assist me again?"

Knowing his sperm would be on display, a humiliated Sean said, "I'll sit this one out."

Tim nodded in understanding. Opening Darcy wider, the step-doctor took a look deep inside her. "We have a problem," he said in disappointment.

"I knew I was the fault! Just go ahead and shoot me now," Darcy said in sadness.

"Relax, Darcy," Stepfather Tim said. "It's nothing like that. It's just...you likely orgasmed extra hard, pushing downward."

Darcy blushed deeply red, "No comment."

The doctor continued. "Anyway...in the process...you ejected too much of his sperm for me to observe your bodily reaction."

"So we do it again?" Sean asked, tightening his ass cheeks.

"No," Tim informed. "I still have your sperm sample. Before you leave, I'll need you to fill another one."

"I can do that," Sean said in anal relief.

Dr. Tim Abel retrieved a sperm vial from the sample refrigerator. He took a rubber tipped syringe, sucking a large sample of sperm into its clear chamber. Once the test tube was empty, he headed back toward the patient.

Slipping the rubber tip into Darcy's tender tunnel, stepfather filled stepdaughter with stepbrother's sperm. He pressed down on the syringe's plunger, watching each cc disappear into Darcy's dripping snatch.

The curvy redhead tensed, trying not to get aroused by her stepbrother's cum coating her insides. A chilled heaviness filled her feminine depths. Just when she didn't think it could fill her more, another load invaded her speculum stretched pussy. Her body shook with lust; gown fell away at the breasts, revealing engorged nipples.

As the last cold shot of semen entered her, Tim Abel tilted the gyno chair. Aiming her butt upward, Darcy's head was lowered to the floor. "I added a little too much...so I'll let that drain for about ten minutes," the doctor said.

Tim sat. The three waited in silent awkwardness, male eyes fixated on Darcy. Her stirrup spread legs remained high in the air. A speculum stretched, cum-filled pussy was on display for their viewing.

After a long ten minutes, Dr. Abel returned Darcy to her seated position. "OK, now we'll need the excess semen to drain," Tim said. "I need you to push like you're going to the bathroom, help speed the emptying process along."

OMG! My stepbrother...husband's load is leaking out of me...while my stepfather watches...and he wants me to help it more! I think I'm in a nightmare! A hot nightmare...but nightmare still!

However her embarrassment, Darcy obeyed her stepfather. She pushed hard, straining every muscle within. A stream of white love seeped out. Contrasting with the pristine pussy, it looked like white paint tossed on a pink canvas, a modern work of art.

Sean looked down in embarrassment. Though his newly hardened cock indicated another force at work. *Not again!* He warned himself.

Shaking in the seat, Darcy kept pushing outward. A bubbling river of stepbrother cum gushed out. The chair edge was soaked in sperm. There was so much, it spilled to the floor.

"Good girl," Tim said. "You can stop now."

Darcy went limp, relaxing her body. She gazed at her stepbrother, staring down at his hard cock. Quite surprised, she suddenly realized he liked it. Dr. Tim Abel stuck a second thinner metal probe through the speculum's border. Aiming all the way back to her cervical wall, he pressed it to Darcy's tight cervical ring.

Grabbing the chair rails, the redhead felt the thin probe enter her cervix. Another clicking sound filled the air, as the tiny speculum opened her tight ring. She moaned and gasped. Stepfather Tim continued without pause. Once the noise stopped, the road to Darcy's womb was fully exposed.

Using the inner light, Dr. Tim Abel took a cotton swab, guiding it deep inside his stepdaughter. As he entered it through the cervical ring, Darcy wiggled at the intense feeling. All the while, clear cervical mucus rushed out, mixed with Sean's sperm.

Tim stuck the cotton swab deeper, swirling and scraping her uterus. The more Darcy squirmed and wiggled, the harder Dr. Abel got. There was something in a patient's submission which turned him on. However, his sexy stepdaughter's submission drove him wild.

Tim removed the swab. He smeared it on a microscope slide. Then, the stepfather mercifully closed and removed the inner speculums from Darcy. "After Sean replaces his sperm sample, both sets of tests will be officially complete. I'll send them to the lab and we'll wait for answers."

"What if...we *can't*?" Sean asked, looking ill.

"Can't...conceive?" Tim responded.

"Right."

"There are many options...in vitro fertilization..."

"No...what I meant to say was...what If *I* can't?" Sean interrupted. "What happens if my sperm isn't good? What if I'm not the man I thought I was?"

"Sean, I told you last time...only 30 percent of the cases are men..."

"Answer me, dad!" Sean insisted.

"For lack of a better answer, Tim said, "Adoption is a fine solution..."

"Fuck!" Sean shouted in frustrated, panicked fear. "I know it's me...my worst fear was always to shoot blanks. My manhood would be crushed...I might as well slap on a dress and call myself Caitlyn!"

Darcy shouted, "Sean Patrick Abel...don't you dare talk like that! You'll always be my man!"

"Son...I don't need to explain to a knowledgeable doctor like yourself...that this happens to many men. It makes them no less of a man!"

Sean rose. "Not *this* man!" he shouted, storming off in fury.

Tim was speechless. He always knew his son was short-fused, though he'd never seen him so defeatist. "We don't even know if he's the cause yet," Dr. Abel said.

"So...what if it's really him?" Darcy asked.

"As I said...adoption..."

"I mean...how will we stop him from losing it?"

Both of them remained silent, staring at each other in worry. Neither of them had an answer, though knew they better find a cure.

*****

Three days passed, the local laboratory sent digital results to Dr. Tim Abel. Upon opening the email, he was pleased to see his stepdaughter's results were excellent for fertility. However, that only left one culprit. With further reading, his worst fears were confirmed. The doctor removed his frameless reading glasses, resting stressed eyes in his hands. "He's screwed!"

Sean Abel *was* the cause of infertility. With a sperm count of 10 million, the odds of egg fertilization were very low. The normal range is 20 million-120 million per millimeter of semen. Although sperm count doesn't make a man, Tim knew his son's alpha pride would destroy him.

However, in vitro was still an option, until Tim read further. Sean's sperm was of poor quality. It was basically, ineffective. The chance of pregnancy would be extremely low. It would break Sean's confidence, his manhood. That was everything to an alpha like him.

Tim was always the one to break the news to patients, though he couldn't destroy the young man. Having lived a life of regret, he didn't want the same for his son. He knew Darcy could handle the news, help break it to Sean. However, there was something more important to tell her first.

It was time to tell Darcy about her mother's death.

*****

"Hey stepdad," the curvy redhead said, hugging Tim Abel. He entered Darcy and Sean's apartment, looking around at the new decor. The walls were painted sage green, little sprigs of fresh flowers were placed throughout.

He also scanned the room for his son. "Sean's...at the office...right?"

"Yeah, booked up today. I can call him, if you want me to. The nurse can flag him down," she said, grabbing her cell phone.

Tim quickly stopped her, "No! I...wanted to come spend time with my daughter. Ever since you moved out, the house has been so quiet."

"I know...it's been strange. It kinda sucks having to make my own breakfast everyday," she smiled. "You spoiled me."

Tim smiled as well, taking another gaze around the room. "Looks good. This place needed a woman's touch. Reminds me of when your..." he paused, finding himself unable to speak the word.

"Mom?" Darcy asked.

"Yes," he said, looking pale, feeling nervous. Although he'd faced risky medical procedures on a daily basis, nothing had shaken his core like the task before him. "Like when *she*...you *both* first moved in. She brought such personality to the place. You have her eye for detail."

"Are you OK, stepdad? You look kinda...green. Can I get you a bottled water?"

"No...no, I'm fine. I promise."

"Oh, then...come here. I've been dying to show someone other than Sean!" she said, leading him by the hand to another room.

Inside the second bedroom, a beautiful display of toys, baby furniture, and a large crib.

Tim turned even more green, feeling sicker. "You haven't even conceived yet."

"I know, but you're gonna help us...right stepdad?"

He exhaled deeply. "Can we talk...in another room? One without...a *crib?*"

Fear filled Darcy's face. "Is the living room OK?"

"Sure."

The two sat down on the couch, Tim tense and crouched. He looked like a man with constipation cramps. "I have some news..."

"We *can't* have children," Darcy said, tears rimming her eyes.

"I wasn't going to say that."

"The look on your face said it for you," Darcy said. Her head sank, a tear rolled down her cheek.

"It's not you."

"Even worse," she said, breaking down in tears.

"At least look into adoption...it's a great thing."

"I'm fine with that, really. But Sean...he's too proud."

Tim put his arm around his stepdaughter, squeezing her tightly. He wiped a tear from her freckled cheek. "I'm so sorry, Darcy. I'd do anything not to see you hurt. Sean either...anything. You're both my children."

"I know, stepdad. I just...always imagined being mother to a newborn. First steps, first words, first smiles...ugh," she shed more tears. "The thing that I *really* wanted...oh forget it...it's so dumb."

"Tell me, please Darcy. Speak your mind."

"If it was a girl...I would've named her Debra...after *mom*," she broke down into her stepfather's chest.

Hearing his deceased wife's name, he was further reminded of his next painful task. *She's distraught, now's not the time to tell her,* he thought. However, he suddenly remembered the therapist's words. *'It's time to tell Darcy the truth. She deserves to know how her mother died, and you deserve to release this secret you've carried around all these years. I know you think avoiding the pain helped you both...but it hasn't.'*

Knowing Shelly Cole was correct, he said, "Darcy...there's something else I have to tell you. It's something you *must* know. Something that may hurt more."

Darcy removed her head from his chest, looking fearful. "Worse than a childless future and broken husband? What could that be?"

"It's about *your* mother. It's something I never told you..."

The redhead's heartbreak was suddenly replaced by shock. "OMG...you poisoned her!"

"What? No! My God...why would you say that?"

"Sorry, I've read too many eBooks. Please...just tell me."

Tim took a deep breath, exhaling even deeper. "The accident...the night she was hit head on...it was by a *drunk* driver."

Darcy turned pale, she trembled. "That's so horrible."

"You can hate me. I won't blame you...I already hate myself for it," he said, rising to leave.

"Stepdad...wait!" she begged, grabbing onto his arm, pulling him back into his seat. She hugged him tightly, "Thank you."

Now Tim was the one in pale shock. "You're thanking me? Why? I hid information from you. It was your right to know."

"Honestly, stepdad...I don't think I could've handled it back then. I was just a kid...my world shattered. Growing up without a mother was hard enough, though knowing she was killed that way...would've broken me. Please, don't hate yourself...you did it to protect me!" she said, hugging the man tighter.

He hugged her back, equally as tight. Like the therapist said, a piece of his heart was healed. Unfortunately, a large majority of it still ached deeply. The ghost, which haunted him, was still present. "I'll always protect you, my red rose." He kissed her on the head.

"Did the guy die too?"

"No...he was barely hurt. He got a slap on the wrist...a liberal fucking judge saying a lack of love from his parents caused him to drink. He was given probation...court ordered to write a letter."

"Are you joking?"

"I couldn't joke about the punk who ruined our lives."

"What did the letter say?"

Dr. Abel pulled a folded letter from his pocket. It was crumbled, taped together. Although a decade had passed, the wear wasn't from time. The damage was from Tim's angry assault upon it. "Read it for yourself. I've read it too many times. It sickens me every time."

Darcy took the shaking letter from her stepfather's hands. Her hands were shaking as much.

The letter read: *Dear Mr. Abel,*

Sorry man, for driving drunk and killing your wife. I usually can handle my liquor, though I guess I was wrong in this case. My car was damaged too, so I lost something too. Anyway, as the court told me to do, I wrote this to say I'm sorry for doing what I did.

Mike Robertson

"Wow! That guy's an asswipe! He could care less about what he did! Why did you keep this? It would make any person bitter!"

Tim's dark face cringed. He thought about her question. "In a sick way...it was my comfort."

"So...you liked it?"

"Oh, no Darcy...not comfort in the way you may think. With every flippant word, my need for revenge was served more."

A look of realization suddenly crossed her face. "That's why you can't move on...it's why you still hurt so much."

"Perhaps," he said, taking the letter back.

Darcy hung on to the letter, refusing to give it back. "Let it go, stepdad. Don't keep torturing yourself. It's not fair to you...to keep living it everyday. At some point, you have to just move on!"

"I need it!" he shouted, pulling at it harder. The letter tore again, Darcy's half floated to the floor. "No!" Tim dove for it, piecing it back together in desperation.

Seeing her stepfather in frantic panic, Darcy ran to get tape. Kneeling to him on the floor, she handed it over. He grabbed it, quickly taping the letter back together, adding yet another layer to the artifact. Once it was reassembled, he placed it to his thumping heart, reclining flat on the floor.

Tears fell from Darcy's eyes, as she lay with him, placing her head upon his chest. "I'm sorry, I didn't mean to rip it."

"It's OK, baby. You're not the one whose sins need resolving. The scumbag took her life...we can never get it back."

"No, we can't, stepdad," Darcy said, placing a hand on her stomach. "I hoped to create another...a life to honor her memory. I guess, that dream's over too."

A flash of determination struck Tim. "Not if I can help it."

"But I thought you said...Sean's sperm couldn't be cured."

"I did."

"Then how can you get me pregnant?"

"Anyway I have to. Do you still trust me...to do the right thing for you?"

"Always."

"Then don't give up. That dream...will come true."

*****

Tim Abel's car pulled up to a decent home in a pleasant neighborhood. No stranger to the sight, it wasn't the first time he'd been there. A few years back, he did an internet search for the drunk driver's name. Knowing his target was 34-years old now, only one matched his criteria. After a visual confirmation, he studied his subject like a scholar to ancient text.

An SUV pulled into the home's driveway. Out walked a man in his mid-thirties. He wore a white shirt and tie. His hair was slicked back, definitely a productive member of society. To the average eye, it was a far cry from a drunken college kid. Nothing physical remained of the slacker's drinking days. Though to Tim Abel, the kid's face was unforgettable. He had a look in his eyes of entitled arrogance. The smirk on his face was ever-present.

Dr. Abel remembered sitting in the courtroom, seeing the drunk's smirk on full display. Even awaiting sentencing, the college kid rolled his eyes in boredom. Throughout, the kid was disinterested. Tim felt like he was in that court again, watching the same spoiled kid walk virtually free.

Upon hearing the sentence, the kid laughed, hugging his high-priced family lawyer. While one family celebrated, another stewed in anger. However, the only family member present was Tim himself. Not even Sean was allowed to go, remaining clueless to the present day.

Tim gazed around at the houses, cringing in sickness. *Pleasantville...a pretty house, trimmed lawn, white picket fence. The guilty fucker gets to live the American dream...while my innocent wife rots in a grave. His kids get to hug their father every day. His wife gets to kiss her husband each night. Why is life so fucking unfair? Why do good people die while scum get to live? He took her from us. Damn it...I'm going to take him from them. Eye for an eye...tooth for a tooth.*

*****

"Hello again, Dr. Abel," Dr. Shelly Cole said, her blond hair sparkling in the bronze room light.

Tim paused momentarily, struck again by the resemblance to his deceased wife. "Hi, Debra...I'm mean, Dr. Cole," he said, shaking her hand. His mind was clearly distracted, face tensed.

"Take a seat."

Tim sat down on the couch. He was uptight, unfocused.

Shelly continued. "So, did we make progress with Darcy?"

"We did," he said in a depressed voice

"You'll have to excuse me Dr. Abel...but the tone of your voice doesn't exactly convey progress."

"It's not *that*...in fact, it couldn't have gone any better. She actually thanked me. I have to admit, Dr. Cole...but...you were right. I should've told her sooner."

The therapist smiled, "I think we're beyond the point of formalities, doctor. Call me, Shelly. May I call you, Tim?"

A surprised, but pleased look crossed Dr. Abel's face. "Please do." He silently wondered, *Does she do this with all her patients...or am I just...special? Oh...special can denote retardation in this field...oh don't be ridiculous. You're a highly educated man!*

"Great. I figure...if I expect a patient to trust me with their innermost thoughts...I can call them by their first name," she said.

The look of hope melted off Tim's face. *Not so special after all. Who was I kidding anyway...therapist's don't date their patients.* "Noted. Shelly it is."

"So, Tim...tell me, what else is troubling you today?"

"It's Darcy...a different issue than the drunk. Actually, it's more my son...than stepdaughter."

"Marital issues?"

"Not of their own making. Fertility trouble."

"I see. Well, I'm not the one to council *you* in that area," Shelly said. Tim smiled at her. Now Shelly was the one to pause, gazing deeply into his eyes.

"Is something wrong, Shelly?"

"No...not at all. Please, go on with your story."

"The thing is...my son doesn't know he's the reason for failure."

"I'm assuming...as his doctor, you'll tell him."

Tim stayed quiet for a moment, looking downward. "I will."

"Is it a fixable issue?"

Again, Dr. Abel paused in hesitation. "I believe it is," he said untruthfully.

"Then fix it."

"I plan on it."

"The look in your eyes tells me...it won't be conventional."

"You're good."

Shelly's mind went to many scenarios, though one seemed impossible yet probable. "I hope I'm not as good as you think...because something tells me...I don't want to know."

"OK, it turns out...you're *really* good. And trust me, you don't."

She hadn't dared speak it in detail. "Do you really think that's wise, doctor?"

"He can't have kids...would never be able to live with failure."

"What's worse...his body failing him...or his father...twice in one life?"

"You wouldn't understand...it's an alpha thing. Pride will kill him well before anything I do."

"Ah...one of those macho men. Very tough nuts to crack. Is he the only reason?"

Tim remained silent for a moment. "Yes."

"Tim...be honest."

"I don't know. Maybe...it's something inside me. Something urging...even begging me to act boldly. I can't explain it."

"Just promise me something, Tim. Whatever it is you're going to do...please, really think it over. It's something you can't undo. Will you ever tell him?"

"I don't know."

"I'd assume Darcy would have to know."

He remained quiet again, "I told you...I'm still undecided on the matter. Haven't thought out the details."

"OK, fair enough. Speaking of Darcy...let's talk about your opening up to her. From the looks of it...it didn't heal your pain."

"I must really look like shit to you."

"No, Tim. I'm reading your emotion...and it tells me you're in pain."

He exhaled in defeat, "Yes, the pain and anger's still there."

"It's OK. We'll keep digging...until that pain goes away."

"But I know the answer...I've known for years. The only question is...should I do it?"

"Do what, Tim?"

He took a deep breath, exhaling afterward. "The dark thoughts."

"Enacting them," she said, fighting her own face from twitching.

"Right...enacting them. He needs to die...for me to live."

Dr. Shelly Cole's face turned pale. Though, the look was less outrage than it was conflict. "Tim...there's nothing wrong with having these thoughts...these fantasies."

"It's not fantasy...once I make it reality. I need to kill him...to avenge my wife! I need to make him hurt...like she hurt! Break every fucking bone in his body...the way her bones were. I need to burn him...the way *she* burned!"

"Years have passed...he may have moved...maybe karma caught up to him...maybe he's dead?"

"Mike Robertson's alive and doing well. Everyday for the last decade...I've gazed at the court ordered letter. His signature...looped letters...big bold print...like some celebrity signing an autograph. Fucking narcissist."

"From the sounds of it...you know more about him than his name, signature. Tell me, Tim…have you been...watching him?"

Dr. Abel's face was flushed, eyes trained to the floor. His voice got darker than it ever had. "I know where he lives...what kind of car he drives...his kids' school...wife's name...the color lipstick she wears on her happy smile..."

"So you're stalking them."

"I'm watching *his* life...the one I never got to have."

"So your mind's made up...you plan on killing him," she stated in a stressed voice.

Tim paused, body tensed like a man in the electric chair. "I can't say."

"Don't know...or can't say?"

"Both. You'll call the authorities."

"Doctor patient confidentiality...I can't...would lose my license."

"In cases of premeditation...we both know *that* privilege is moot."

"Then I *won't!*" she boldly and convincingly declared.

"Why not?"

Shelly's heart raced, pulse pounded, clear streams of sweat wet her skin. She ignored his question. "Will taking his life heal your pain?"

"I'm beyond the point of lectures, Shelly. As a therapist...I know it's your job to talk me out of it..."

"I'm *not* talking you out of it. I'm asking you...will it heal your pain?"

Shock crossed Tim's face. "Aren't you the shrink here?"

"Even the best therapists...lack answers vital to their own lives. We're still human beings."

"How's my situation vital to your life?"

"I lost my husband," she admitted.

"I'm so sorry to hear that...truly. But...what does *that* have to do with my need for vengeance? Could you enlighten me on that?"

A streak of shame struck Shelly. *Oh my God...I've committed the unthinkable therapist sin. I've become the patient!* "I'm sorry, Tim...I need to cut this session short," she said, standing.

Another look of surprise filled Tim's face. Though intrigue was the greater emotion. He stood up, saying, "I'm sorry, Shelly. I didn't mean to..."

"No…it's me, not you. Though, I have to say…I don't think the first name thing was a good idea. We should return to our respective titles."

"OK, Dr. Cole. Can I just ask…"

"Dr. Abel…I'm the one who's supposed to ask the questions. Now please, sir…I must end this session for today."

"When should I return?"

"When I ask you to," she said, shuffling through old paperwork, avoiding eye contact.

Finally getting the message, Tim headed for the door. Before exiting, he stopped. "Whatever I said to offend you…I'm sorry."

"I'm the one who's sorry, doctor," she said, failing to offer further detail.

With those last words, Tim Abel exited her office. He never expected to see her again, though it didn't matter. His mind was already made up. *I know what I must do to end this pain.*

I need to end one life…and create another.

CHAPTER FOUR

"Put on the gown and sit in the chair. Dr. Abel will be right in to see you," the nurse told Darcy in the exam room.

The redhead's eyebrows rose in surprise. "No, he just...wanted to talk...I think."

"I just follow the doctor's instructions, Mrs. Abel. He said to put on the gown and get in the chair. That's all I know," the nurse said, exiting the room.

Why would he do that? He already examined me...my results came back fine. Did he find a way to cure Sean's problem? He promised that I'd carry the Abel seed...no matter what he had to do. Oh shit! He's an Abel too. Na...he'd never do that. I mean, Sean would lose his mind. Though...I doubt he'd be as heart broken as a childless future. Maybe...he'd never even know. Stepdad looks like an older version of Sean, the resemblance would be similar. I can't say I'd mind having sex with him...as the anal was damn good. AM I

NUTS? He'd never ask such a thing anyway! Grow up, Darcy...this is crazy talk!

Forcing thoughts from her head, she removed her clothes. Slipping the paper gown over feminine curves, she sat in the gyno chair. Waiting nervously, she bit her bottom lip in fear. As a knock sounded on the door, her anxiousness only grew more.

Entering the room, he paused at the mere sight of his stepdaughter. It wasn't her appearance that spooked him. He feared what he had to do. "Hello Darcy," he finally said, walking over to hug her. It had been a few weeks since her last test, timed to the day by the ovulation calendar.

The look in Tim's eyes spoke louder than his voice. It was as if he'd told her his plan without speaking. Their thoughts synced, even though they hadn't quite processed it yet. "Hi stepdad," Darcy said.

"You're probably wondering why I called you here...asked you to wear a gown."

"It's OK, stepdad," she said. "It doesn't matter why. Just...save us. Save Sean from himself."

Empowerment seized Dr. Abel's face. Darcy's words cemented his plan, all but granting verbal permission to enact it. *I can't let her carry the blame...burden of hiding a lifelong secret. I'll carry it for her.* Without speaking, he headed over to a cabinet. He removed something, slipping it in his pocket. Darcy didn't see what it was. "I told Sean...just minutes ago," he said.

"You did?" she asked in shock. "Did he freak out? He must be hurting right now, angry, embarrassed to know the truth..."

"I didn't tell him the truth."

"No?"

"I told him his results were fine...like his wife. I lied."

"So he'll just keep trying...and failing? Is that really the answer, stepdad?"

Tim slowly approached Darcy. "Put your feet in the stirrups," he said in a dominant tone.

Darcy's heart pounded. She wondered what was going to happen. Although scared, she hoped for him to seed her. *I know this is so wrong...soooo wrong! But...it will save Sean...plus make my dream come true. My husband can't be fixed. I can lie to myself and say I don't want to feel my stepfather inside my pussy...but it would be pointless. I do want it. He felt amazing in my ass...his cum did too. Will I ever be able to forgive myself for allowing it?* Darcy obediently put her feet in the stirrups, parting her thighs like Moses' did the Red Sea. With her feminine feet firmly in the stirrups, Darcy awaited action.

One last exhale exited Tim's lungs. Shifting all thoughts of consequence aside, he felt her forehead. Removing a glass thermometer, he lubed the tip, along with her asshole. As it was slipped into her sphincter, Darcy squirmed in the chair.

After waiting a minute, he removed the glass probe from the dark garden. Studying it, his timing was right on. *A slight rise in temperature...she's ovulating again. It's now or never.*

Next, he opened an alcohol swab. Cleansing her ass cheek with one hand, he carefully removed a syringe from his pocket. Hiding it behind his medical coat, he neared his stepdaughter.

Finally ready to end the anxious wonderment, Darcy asked, "Can I ask...what you plan on doing to me, stepdad?"

Without speaking another word, Tim Abel jabbed the needle's spear into Darcy's ass cheek. Spread in the gyno chair, Darcy moaned loudly. "What are you doing...step...dad!" she slurred, feeling the heavy rush of medicine squirt into her. Her eyelids fought to stay open, fluttering. "Stepdad...I feel kinda dizzy," she said in a whispered voice.

"Shhh." Darcy's stepfather placed a latex finger to her full lips. "Just let the medicine take you away. Surrender your total submission to me...and I'll save you both."

"Please...tell me why," her breathy voice gushed. Darcy's eyeballs rolled upwards, last signs of lucidness faded. "I'm so sleepy."

"Shhh," he said again, covering her mouth, pinching her nostrils. The lack of oxygen helped her float faster into twilight. He knew she'd first enter a stage of true sleep. Within minutes, she'd exit from slumber, feeling every sexual stroke with heightened pleasure. She'd remain confused, eventually awakening to a cloudy reality.

Tim thought, *She deserves to experience her journey into motherhood, even if it feels like a dream. She never asked me to do this...therefore...she'll never have to live with the guilt accompanying the aftermath.*

Darcy's lids closed. Her body went fully limp as she officially entered the sleep stage. Feet remained propped in the stirrups, legs spread. Her stepfather leaned inward, kissing her forehead.

Dr. Abel lowered his pants, freeing an 8-inch cock of steel. Tossing all guilt aside, a hunger to seed his stepdaughter outweighed all emotion. He walked towards her smooth thighs, sliding his cock-head along her sleepy slit.

His thick member engorged more, girth expanded in arousal. Every vein popped in strain, begging to feel Darcy's creamy pussy. He placed the bulbous head against her honey hole, pushing inward. In moments, his manly helmet popped into the poon paradise.

A satisfied moan sounded from Dr. Abel. With Darcy asleep, her vaginal tension completely relaxed. However, the deeper he sank into her, the closer her 19-year-old natural tightness hugged his rod.

Soon, all 8-inches were inside her. Tim's face tensed from the unbelievable pleasure. Not only was the sensation soft and sensual, but also a dream come true. After anally pleasing her on his marital bed, he'd planned to claim her pussy. However, he'd erupted, missing his chance. Ever since that night, he'd imagined the feeling. His wish was granted.

He began fucking her, slow steady strokes. His cock was awash in her sweetness. With each passionate entrance, he stared at her resting face. It was so beautiful, so peaceful. Her lips were so wet and full.

The mere sight of her limp curvy body made him harder. Of course, the fact that she was helpless to his sexual whims drove him wild. Chemical chains kept her prisoner to his sexual orders.

His forward slides turned to crashes. Darcy's body jolted from the landings. Tim held her ankles in the stirrups, keeping her safely in-place. His balls spanked stepdaughter ass cheeks, ramming his hardness as deeply as possible.

Still staring at her lips, he had to kiss them. Leaning inward, he kept his fucking motion moving. Stepfather's lips engulfed stepdaughter's. The set on her mouth were as sweet as her pussy flaps. After just one peck, Darcy's body began to gently rouse.

Her sleepy lips fought to return the loving gesture. It couldn't, though Dr. Abel performed enough for them both. Lip locks transformed into French kissing. Passion filled Darcy's partially conscious body. It began to regain some control, her tongue joined in on the action. Together, stepfather and stepdaughter did the forbidden dance.

Feeling his cock swell, Dr. Abel broke the kiss. He stood straight again, pounding away at his stepdaughter's pink pussy. Even though cumming was the purpose of his mission, he fought from doing so. *This is the only time I'll ever get to do this. I don't want it to end...I must hold on! It feels too damn good!*

Needing a distraction, he turned to Darcy's feminine feet. Licking the sole of her right foot, he rose up the sensitive center. His fucking rhythm remained steadily hard, tongue licked and sucked on her foot. He engulfed her toes with his mouth, biting each one. Tim crashed harder into her.

The first sounds of pleasure trickled from Darcy's captive mouth. A ghostly tickle fluttered through her body, teasing her partially conscious mind. Thick cock invaded her dreams, as a pleasurable ache dragged her from drugged sleep itself.

Darcy's eyelids gently opened. *Is this even real?* She wondered. *Am I dreaming? I'm so confused...I just know I want more. It feels so good, I want my stepfather to own me...knock me up.* The sleeping beauty shut her eyes again, lost in a sexual fog.

Dr. Abel's manly member pounded deeper into the redhead's pussy. Darcy was so wet and creamy, her love juice dripped down his swinging balls. Reaching out for her breasts, Tim grabbed handfuls of the C-cups. Tugging and pulling on erect nipples, electric pulses of pained-pleasure shot through her body. He smashed his stepdaughter's velvet tunnel with more vigor. Switching to the left foot, his saliva spilled down it.

His hands worked her breasts like manic marionettes. The crazed sensations further awakened Darcy's senses. Feeling the cock ram her deepest vaginal depths, her pussy was inflamed with sexual fire.

Darcy's arousal built like a slow-moving tsunami. Many small waves of pleasure united in an unworldly splash. With one last cock blow, the redheaded stepdaughter erupted in erotic explosion. In her head, she screamed louder than she ever had before, orgasming to a level never experienced.

She felt herself rumble, shake, and grab onto the chair rails. Warm chills crossed her sweaty skin, feeling her stepfather's cock continuously pound her pussy. Darcy felt her voice speak, "Stepdad...cum inside me! Give me your baby!"

Of course, she didn't actually make a sound or movement. Captive to chemical sleep, the ballet of lust remained trapped inside her pleasurable poon prison. Though her verbal muzzle didn't matter. Her unspoken request was about to be fulfilled.

"Fuck!" Dr. Abel shouted, freeing Darcy's cute feet from his mouth. Her wet, teenage pussy choked and milked his cock, nearly begging for cum itself. He drove into her, forced to fire his heavy white load.

His deep manly grunt filled the air. His white medical coat floated behind him in the air-conditioned breeze, muscular ass cheeks stiffened. The 54-year-old stepfather filled his 19-year-old stepdaughter with a forbidden flood.

Darcy reached the fine line between sleep and control, her body shook violently. Feeling her stepfather's seed made her orgasm again, harder than the first. Each load felt bigger than the last, squirted hard and deep into her womb. The more it filled her, the more cum she craved.

Tim Abel's balls were nearly drained of life, firing every single sperm they could produce. A ring of white formed around the base of his cock and Darcy's pussy lips. There was so much, it overflowed.

After his last squirt coated the curvy patient, he quickly withdrew. Darcy's eyes jolted open, free from twilight. However, a surprised stab of the syringe's needle returned her to darkness.

The captive dream-state continued on. Tim would claim her womb again and again, shooting Abel sperm deep into the sexy redhead. The stepfather had successfully seeded his stepdaughter's womb. More importantly, Darcy would never have to face the guilt of consenting to it.

Finally able to ejaculate no more, the step-doctor adjusted the stirrups. Bringing the steel spreaders tightly together, he shut Darcy's legs, trapping his cum inside her fertile womb. Then, he lowered her gyno chair downward, tilting it at a diagonal angle. Her head was aimed at the floor, pussy in the air. The frothing cum was forced downward into the womb. It forced the army of white life through the cervical ring, into the uterus, and right for the ovary's bulls eye.

By the time Darcy awoke with a gasp, she was being watched by the nurse. Returned to an upright, seated position and dressed in her clothes, confusion overcame her. "Stepdad?"

"He's with another patient. I'll walk you out," the nurse said.

The redhead nodded, following the nurse to the exit. *What happened in here? My mind is so hazy. Did he really have sex with me...or was it just a dream? I couldn't ask him...would be too embarrassing. Was it as hot as it felt? Did he really knock me up? Is it wrong that I remember liking it?*

Is it wrong...that I hope it was real?

*****

Dr. Shelly Cole kissed her husband's cheek. She was sitting next to him in the passenger seat. Darkness and fog masked the chilly night. Headlight beams were swallowed by thick atmosphere.

"I love you so much, handsome," she said, gazing at her husband lovingly.

"Not as much as I love you, beautiful," he responded, keeping his eyes responsibly on the road ahead.

"We'll call it a tie," she declared with a smile.

"I'd call that fair. Though, I swear to you...that love will never die." His voice seeped with passion.

Shelly's husband's words skipped her ears, heading straight for the heart. A warmth surrounded her, mesmerized by his deep love. "Mine either. Though...can you make room for one more?"

He gasped. "You're...pregnant?"

"I am," she said with a beaming smile.

A quick turn of his head met her lips. "I'll love you both with all my heart...on this earth and after."

Suddenly, a pair of headlights shot through the fog, getting brighter with each moment. "A car's...coming...at us..."

CRASH! It happened in a flash of a moment, though to Shelly's eyes, it appeared to never end. Time slowed to a death crawl. A pickup truck roared through fog like a ghost train. Shelly and husband were traveling at the speed limit of 65 MPH. The truck barreled forward at 100 MPH.

The collision was punishing, impact horrifying. They hit so hard, steel bent like hammered butter. While the truck's engine remained intact, Shelly's Toyota engine was crushed.

Though as bad as the outside damage was, the inside impact was deadly. Too frightened to scream, the couple froze in suspended disbelief. Glass shattered inward, peppering them with dagger-like shards.

Each of their bodies were hurled forward, yanked upon like rag dolls. Although seat belts protected the couple from being ejected, the force broke bones instantly. Shelly saw the massive truck heading to crush her.

Right before the vehicle could end her life, the car took a rip-roaring spin. Her husband turned the car away from her, towards himself. The truck's weight was shifted towards his side, crushing the dashboard into his chest. Speeding forward, the offensive vehicle shoved Shelly's car off road, into an old oak tree.

A piece of metal debris hit Shelly Cole in the forehead. Everything went black, though her ears remained in operation. The sound of more grinding steel was heard. Her car was pulled forward in motion. It spun out again, as if flung by the hand of a giant. The dark, terrifying ride was like a deadly *Space Mountain*. Another loud bang shook her, finally stopping. Then, the sound of a rusty dying engine drove off.

Shelly's eyes opened as if awakening from a nightmare. She gazed out the glassless window, on the opposite roadside of her blackout. The sound of distant sirens filled the air.

Reality started to drift back. The nightmare was real. Quickly turning her head, she was face to face with her dead husband. Shaking in traumatic fear, she tried to scream, though only air came out. One of her husband's eyes was out of socket, a trail of blood spilled from his open mouth. A glass dagger pierced his throat. Though the worst thing of all: a metal rod impaled his loving heart.

"AHHHH!" Shelly screamed in traumatic horror. She was not covered in blood, but sweat. The professional therapist wasn't facing her husband, but a ghostly memory. Dr. Cole wasn't in a destroyed car, she was in her bedroom. Although she wasn't currently living a nightmare, she'd already lived it.

The night terrors were nothing new, they reoccurred every night. Each one felt more real, each detail more chilling. For a moment, she reached out to touch her deceased husband's face, swearing he was physically there. Though he'd just disappear like liquid smoke.

She rolled off the bed, landing in a fetal position. "Go away...make me forget...take the pain with you!" she cried. The more she begged, the stronger her memories played on.

First it was her being welded out of the steel coffin of car. Then came the cutting of her seat belt. She remembered grabbing onto the strap, begging the EMT workers, "Please...let me stay with him. He needs me! My husband needs me! The baby needs its father!" The medics had to pry her hands off the strap, wrestle her from the car, and strap her to the gurney.

She recalled seeing her husband's blood-covered body. The horrific sight continued, as he was cut and freed from the driver's seat. As his torso was removed, his legs were severed. The bent steering column had cut his body in two.

Then her memories skipped to the hospital. The doctors entered, unable to stare her in the face. "I've lost the baby," she said coldly, emotionlessly.

"I'm sorry, Mrs. Cole...we believe it was the force from the seatbelt...though it's too hard to say for sure. We're sorry for your losses," he said. "We'll provide grief therapy..."

"I *am* a therapist," she said in a deep monotone voice. Clearly, shock set in, turning all emotion off. "There's nothing they can tell me...that I don't already know. Leave me alone."

"I'll give you some time," he said, turning to exit with his team.

"Doctor," she said.

The man stopped, turning to address her. "Yes, Mrs. Cole?"

"I need to know...what happened to the man who hit us?"

The doctor paused. "He's dead. We found his demolished vehicle down the road. He drove into another tree," he said, turning to leave again.

"He was drunk," she said as a matter of fact.

"Get some rest. We'll talk about that later..."

"Tell me. It's my right to know."

The doctor stopped, keeping his back to her. "He was."

Shelly's flashback ended there. Curled in a ball on her bedroom floor, tears fell from her eyes like acid rain. Learning the driver was drunk was as painful as the loss itself. "My family died for nothing!" she screamed. "I wanted revenge! I was owed it, damn it! Owed something!" She broke down in manic hurt.

The usual suicidal thoughts plagued her, though one thing had kept her going through the years: vengeance. It seemed impossible for her to get, since the drunk died before *she* could. However, it suddenly became obtainable again. It wasn't her direct target, though a scumbag nonetheless. The therapist in her knew it was wrong, though the wife needed it.

Shelly Cole came to a decision. She wiped her tears again, stood tall, and clinched her fists. "The bastard must die for his sins. For Tim's pain...and my own."

*****

Dr. Tim Abel lay in bed. Weeks expired since seeding his stepdaughter, they hadn't spoken since. During the span of time, many thoughts crossed his mind. *Will my seed take hold? Does she even know I did it? Does she hate me for doing it? Will she ever tell my son?*

However, his usual obsession also grew greater. He gazed at pictures of the drunk driver's house. Although he photographed it a few years ago, the image brought him comfort when unable to stalk in person. Having walked the building's perimeter, he timed when the home was occupied and vacant. Work was 9-5 on weekdays, usually running 10 minutes late. Wife and kids left at 8 AM, were home at 6 PM, often on schedule.

It gives me an hour...morning or night. An hour to kill, he thought in his mind. *Then...I can deal with his wife and kids.* A chill crossed his skin, fright seized his body. It wasn't the thought of taking lives which scared him; it was his lack of remorse which did. His dark thoughts started feeling normal. Killing his enemy felt more holy than letting him live. There was no turning back. Teetering on the very edge of action, all he needed was a slight push.

A sudden knock at the door startled him. He looked at the clock, wondering, *Who the hell would be knocking at 3 AM? Darcy or Sean would likely call.* Rising from the bed, he crept to the front entrance. Turning on the light, he peeked through the peephole. *OK...this is likely a dream. Wet dream, perhaps?* He wondered in hope.

He opened the door, expecting to awaken. Instead, he was greeted by his guest. "Hello, Tim," Shelly Cole said. "May I come in?"

The speechless Dr. Abel nodded, having no words. The sexy blond therapist entered, as he followed her inside. "How'd you..."

"Your medical history forms...the line that said address."

"I should've figured. The question I should really ask...why are you here? Why at this time?"

"I'm sorry...this was incredibly rude, impulsive, and unprofessional. I could lose my license for this. I'll go," she said, heading towards the door.

The strong older man grabbed her arm. He pulled her into him forcefully, the two crashed together. Their eyes met, lips neared. A magnetic force nearly drew them. "You're not going anywhere," he declared.

Used to holding and needing the power, Dr. Shelly Cole suddenly felt like the submissive patient. "OK, doctor...I'll stay."

He kept hold of her, unwilling to let go. "So tell me...why here, why now?"

"Because I had to answer the question...my own question," she said.

"What question? What couldn't wait until a decent hour?" Tim asked in confusion.

"Will killing *him* heal *your* pain?" she recited.

Tim's face grew tense. "Will it?"

She looked him dead in the eyes, heated with anger. She boldly said, "It'll heal *our* pain."

"Our?"

Shelly exhaled, "I told you I lost my husband. I never told you...it was the same way you lost your wife. I lost my unborn child with him. I saw unspeakable horror unfold before my eyes."

A look of deep pain filled Tim Abel. "I'm so sorry."

"The fault doesn't belong to you. You're a victim...as I am," she stated. "I spent years in my therapy practice trying to answer this very question...I couldn't find it. Though when you walked in...everything changed. This *has* to be the way. We can't bring them back. We can't resurrect life...though damn it...we can take it."

Tim finally had clarity in his mind. The last blockade to vengeance was gone. Shelly looked at Tim, waiting for a response. He stared into her eyes, grabbing the back of her blond head. Pulling her into him, he kissed her lips passionately. The feeling was amazing to them both. It was like a fire of love, once snuffed, was suddenly rekindled. Hit like a bolt of lightning, both of them pulled away. Unsure and afraid of the pulsing pound inside their hearts, they returned their focus to the matter at hand.

Forcing the feelings away, Shelly asked, "How will you do it? Fists? A knife? A gun?"

A new shade of darkness crossed Dr. Abel's face. "Anything I can get my hands on."

Shelly shut her eyes, hoping beyond words that it would cure her pain. If it didn't, not only would she be an accessory to murder, she'd have led her patient to commit it. At that moment, neither of them cared about consequence. They wanted revenge, and at 5 PM, they'd have it. "Do you have room for one more weapon?" she asked.

"Like what?"

"Me."

CHAPTER FIVE

Dr. Abel's car pulled up to the drunk driver's home. The low winter sun neared its early set time. Tim gazed at his watch, seeing the hands form 5 o'clock. With a usual ten-minute window, he awaited his prey's arrival.

Both Shelly and Tim sat silently. The blond therapist stared at Tim's bag, seeing an iron-poker, blowtorch, scalpel, rope, and a can of gasoline. For all her vengeful fantasizing over the years, reality felt much different.

The therapist's inner-voice begged her, *You must stop this. The blood will be on your hands. You took an oath, have a responsibility to uphold. Instead, you betrayed it. Shut up!* Shelly's dark side took-over. *You owe this to* your husband...*to yourself. Killing this piece of shit will make things right, allow you to sleep at night. Make him suffer like you suffered!* Forcing all thoughts from her mind, Shelly asked, "Shouldn't we go inside before he gets home? Take him by surprise?"

"They've got a house alarm. He only arms it when no one's home...and when he sleeps at night. Don't worry, he takes a shower immediately after work."

"You certainly know him well."

"A predator must find its prey's weakness and strength before attacking. It's crucial to success."

Shelly nodded, "I guess I've never...actually hunted human before."

Another minute of tense silence passed. Tim asked, "How were you able to move on...after seeing such things? I mean, I had a stepdaughter to cling to, a son...but you lost everything."

Shelly was quiet, exhaling before speaking. "I may appear physically here to you, doctor...but understand this...I never left *that* vehicle. I died there alongside my family. Yes, I was alone...I'm still alone. I hide within. I wanted a child so badly, though couldn't betray my husband like that."

"Did you try to date?"

"How could I love again...when I can lose it all as easily? Emotional investment takes everything...and I have nothing to deposit."

"So you're no different than I am."

"Sadly, I'm not."

"Should you really be charging me then?"

A sly smirk crossed Shelly's face. "Consider it on the house, doctor."

The sun sank, darkness barely kissed sky. A pair of headlights shined, as a car pulled into the enemy's home.

"It's time," Tim said, locking his eyes on the prey.

*****

Mike Robertson let the water cascade his freshly shaven face. Shiny clean, he stepped up to the mirror's reflection, flashing his pearly white veneers. After lotioning his skin, he gelled his hair back. The high-maintenance man valued his appearance above all else in life. The only glare in his dark eyes was vanity, remorse unknown to them.

Blowing a kiss to his reflection, he repeated, "Number one," holding a finger up. If anything was clear about him, he was as much a douchebag as his younger days. Exiting the room, he headed into the kitchen. Opening up the refrigerator, he grabbed a Corona beer. As he closed the swinging door, a stranger appeared behind it.

Crack! A fist flew at his face. Pained moans sounded from the 34-year-old as he crashed to the ground. The bottle smashed beside him. Beer suds sprayed his body, stung his eyes. A few glass shards pierced his skin. Wiping his eyes clear, Mike the drunk, saw Tim standing over him. Shelly stood behind Tim.

Dr. Abel held the iron fireplace poker; Shelly Cole dangled a line of rope from her hand. The panicked Mike Robertson grabbed the broken beer bottle. He swung it at Tim's leg. Alert and focused, Tim swung the metal poker, blocking and smashing the glass bottle toward the enemy.

Then he whacked Mike's hand with the iron rod, breaking the remaining bottleneck in the punk's palm. The drunk driver screamed in pain, glass cracking inside hand, bones breaking as well. Tim Abel raised the poker, finally ready to smite the demon.

Desperate and afraid, the drunk driver kicked Tim's knees. Dr. Abel fell backwards, dropping the poker. The younger guy leapt on the older doctor, swinging at his face. "You fucker!" he shouted, continuing to bludgeon his mystery assailant.

WHACK! The iron poker hit drunken Mike's head. The arrogant enemy was knocked back, flung off Tim. Before the doctor could recover, Shelly continued the assault. First she hit his nose with the iron weapon, breaking it. Swinging wildly, she hit the man in the ribs. "Die! Die! Die! Let our pain die with you!" she shouted, crying her eyes out. Even then, her assault continued, years of frustration and anger flowing. She kept swinging until collapsing.

Dr. Abel caught her fall, hugging her tightly. "It'll all be over soon…but not yet," he said with cold assurance in his voice.

Hearing Tim's words, the bloodied drunk driver desperately crawled away. "Fuck off!" he yelled, slipping on his own blood.

"I'm going to need the rope," he told Shelly, gently setting her down. Taking the line, Tim pursued his fleeing prisoner.

Shelly broke down in deeper tears, realizing that her pain hadn't dissolved at all. *It's not gone like I hoped. Will killing him finally do it? I know better than this…I've seen past victims…it didn't work for them. Why me? How will I live with it? How will Tim live with it? It's too late now…he's on a mission…and no one can stop him.*

Tim slowly trailed his prey, walking the crimson path. The drunk driver's trembling hand reached for the doorknob. Right before he could touch it, the rope was wrapped around Mike's neck.

Yanked away from escape, Tim secured the enemy's slicked, stiffened hair. Dragged back to a kitchen chair, the drunk was forcefully bound to the structure. The arrogant man spit blood out at Tim. Instead of wiping it, Dr. Abel merely smeared it on his cheeks, like war paint.

Shelly watched in wonderment. *Is he losing his mind...or just trying to make the man think he's lost it?*

Another closed fist hit Mike's eye, immediately swelling it shut. The enemy let out a pained shout. "Why the fuck are you doing this? You want money? Man, I got plenty of it. I'll give you all of it...just fucking let me go."

A crazed laugh sounded from Tim Abel. Once a usually reserved man, years of bottled up anger were unleashed. Although he melted down after facing his feelings for Darcy, it was now way beyond that. He was losing all control of himself. The taunting laughter continued for minutes straight, getting louder and crazier. "You think this is about money?" Tim shouted.

"I don't give a fuck what it is, asswipe! I'll have the cops bust your ass either way!" Mike said arrogantly. Even in an imprisoned, pained state, he still acted with no concern.

Tim's laughter stopped, as he ran to his bag of pain. First he removed a small pastry blowtorch. Handing it to Shelly, he said "Light it up...hold it outward...away from you."

She obeyed, holding the shaking flame a distance away. Tim held the iron poker to the red fire. The dark metal turned orange, sizzling on its surface. Small sparks began spitting from it.

Hearing and smelling the evidence, Mike shouted, "What the fuck are you doing?"

Taking his time, Tim made sure it got hotter. Walking back to the tied man, Dr. Abel waved the poker at the drunk driver's face. "Call the cops. I'd write you a letter...but after I burn your eyes out...you won't be able to read it!" he shouted, forcing the hot poker at the douchebag's eye. Mike shut his lid, getting it burned. A high-pitched scream sounded, feeling his lid slowly disintegrate. Tim removed it before touching cornea.

Mike cursed and cried, shouting, "Take whatever the fuck you want! Leave me alone!"

"Oh...I'm going to take exactly what I came here for. I'll take your life...after dismantling you limb from limb. Then...I'll burn you alive."

"You sick fuck!" Mike screamed.

Shelly gasped at Tim's dark words. The vengeful fantasy finally became real. Already disgusted by her uncharacteristic acts of violence, she no longer believed killing was the cure to their pain at all. However, it was too late to turn back.

Tim continued, "Sick? I've been sick for the last ten years, you snot-nosed spoiled fuck!" he yelled, sticking the hot poker on Mike's balls. Although covered, the cloth quickly burned away. Each layer removed, searing pain filled the flailing man. It sizzled testicle skin, branding the drunk's manhood like marked cattle. Tim removed it before burning deeper.

"Ahhhhh! My nuts...my fucking nuts!" he cried out in frantic horror. "I didn't do anything!" He continued shedding tears and screaming.

Aligning his face with the drunk driver, Tim said, "You don't even remember my face."

"I've never seen you before, asshole! You got the wrong fucking man."

"Look at me, you piece of scum!" Tim screamed loudly. His face was red, veins popped from within, spit speckled outwardly.

"Water me down please! I told you, I don't fucking know you!"

"There you were in the courtroom...arrogant smirk on your face...twiddling your fucking thumbs without a care in the world. A man sat across from you...his eyes burning into your soul-less gaze. You looked over once...after the verdict was read, smirking even more. You got away with murder...you got a away with killing my wife!"

The beaten, bloodied man gasped. "You! You're the husband! The dude I wrote the letter to. I apologized for the accident like I had to."

"There was no fucking accident!" Tim screamed, head-butting the punk hard.

Cringing in pain, the guy shouted, "It's not like I meant to kill her."

"You had two DUI's before it! Still...you drove drunk!"

"What do you want from me, asshole? You got the letter!"

A big smile crossed Tim's face. "I want you to suffer...in the exact way I once did."

"How?"

"By denying you what I never had. Your wife and kids will be home in an hour. I'll load them in the car...drive them into a fucking wall!"

Shelly gasped, realizing Tim had lost it. She didn't care about saving Mike's life, it was Tim she had to save from himself. *He's becoming...the thing he hates the most!*

"You piece of shit! My family has nothing to do with this!" Worry and fear painted Mike's face. The arrogance was momentarily lifted from him, clearly hit in his weakest spot.

Rage filled Tim, as he grabbed pictures off the walls. One by one, he held them in Mike's face. The first was a family picture with the kids "Memories!" he shouted, smashing the glass frame the picture was in. Next was a picture of Mike and his wife on the beach, kissing. Tim smashed another one. "Love!" He went on a rampage, smashing every picture they had. "You robbed me of all this!"

"Don't do this, man...please," Mike begged, crying.

"Aww...the scumbag's sad! The scumbag's hurt! Suddenly, when it's his life about to be destroyed, he cries. Do you know how many fucking tears I've cried, you maggot!" he shouted, hurling another fist into Mike's face.

Mike's tears stopped immediately. Clearly, they were false. It was the last straw for Tim Abel. He ran for the gasoline can. Opening the cap, he began soaking his prey to burn alive.

"Help! Someone help me...someone...*GURGLE*..." Tim poured gas into the enemy's mouth. Mike quickly spit it out, gagging up a storm.

Shelly shook in fear, watching in disbelief. In control of the blowtorch, she was the one thing standing between life and death, vengeance and guilt, rationality and rage.

After the can was empty, Tim approached Shelly. Holding out his hand, Tim said, "It's time to end this. It's time to heal our pain."

"This isn't the way, Tim."

"What? You agreed..."

"I thought it would...prayed it would...but all this...healed nothing inside me. Examine your heart...is your pain gone? I hurt every bit as much. He'll get his karma...just not by *our* hands."

Tim paused, feeling the same pain sting his soul. However, he refused to believe it wasn't the answer. In his mind, it was his last chance. "He's not dead yet...we won't know until it's done...until he's a pile of ash."

"No! You sick bastard!" Mike shouted.

Shelly implored Tim, "We can't take this back if we're wrong."

"I can live with that," he said, searching the kitchen cabinets, pulling out drawers. He found what he was seeking. "Matches!" he shouted, holding up the box like a proud father with a newborn.

He removed a match, as Shelly stepped in front of the tied prisoner. "Don't become him, Tim. The moment he dies...we'll become the men who killed our spouses. We'll become the people we hate the most."

"Shelly, I can't live with this pain anymore, regret. I have to make it stop...somehow...someway. If becoming him saves me...then it's a small price to pay," he said, walking past Shelly.

"Just fucking listen to her, bro! I won't tell anyone about this! I swear! Just let me go!"

Tim shoved a nearby cloth napkin into Mike's mouth. "Shut up!"

Her body slumped as she turned her back to the sight. She couldn't watch, hearing Tim strike the match against the box's side. Shelly waited for the sting of hot flames, crackle of snapping fire, scent of burnt flesh, and deathly scream of the drunk driver.

To her surprise, a familiar song filled her ears instead. The sound was nearby, stuck down inside the bag. It was a ringtone from Tim's phone, specific to one caller. A soft trumpet played a calming melody, contrasting the furious situation. *La Vie en Rose*, representing the girl he loved the most.

Holding the flickering flame in-hand, Tim badly needed to end the drunk driver's life. He shamefully felt like Darcy was watching him do it. However, not even *that* could stop him.

"Get ready to burn in hell," Tim said to Mike, letting the matchstick slip from his fingers.

An unexpected voice suddenly made him stop. "Dad?"

To his shock, Tim recaptured the match. He turned to see Shelly holding the phone. She hit speaker, remembering hearing Darcy's ringtone during the therapy session. Knowing the redhead brought light to his life, Shelly took the risk.

"Darcy...I'll have to call you back...I'm in the middle of a heated situation. You're..."

"...Pregnant," Darcy's tearful voice said, hijacking his sentence.

A surreal feeling struck Tim Abel. It was as if his rage suddenly lifted. Even standing there, holding vengeance itself, he nearly forgot about the scumbag in front of him.

"Dad?" Darcy asked again. "Are you OK?"

"I am, baby," he said, his voice breaking up from his own tears. The man began sobbing, uncontrollably. He dropped to his knees. "I *truly* am...my red rose," he said, further breaking down.

Shelly erupted in tears as well, leaning downward, ending the call. She blew out the match in Tim's hand, ensuring he didn't drop it. Shelly asked, "What made you stop?"

"I found it," he said in hysterics. "I finally found it!"

"Found what?"

"The cure...to losing life...losing love."

"Tell me...what is it?" she begged.

"Creating it," he said, gazing deeply in Shelly Cole's eyes.

Without another word spoken, the two lunged for each other. Their tongues danced, hands and faces were speckled with tears and stains of revenge. The drunk driver's swollen eyes watched in disbelief. Soaked in gasoline, cut, bruised, burned and broken, the scumbag wasn't going anywhere.

Still full of adrenaline and aggression, Tim Abel tore at Shelly Cole's clothes. Having created life once *that* night, he ached to do it again. At 40 years of age, the therapist was still fertile. With Darcy as living proof, at 55, Tim's sperm still swam.

Tim tore at the blond's clothes, lifting her shirt above the breasts. Next, he yanked on her bra, freeing a set of D-cups. Like a hungry beast, he gnawed upon tender feminine flesh. He bit a trail downward to rock hard nipples. The doctor switched between teeth and tongue, stimulating Shelly with pain and pleasure.

Having only been with a vibrator in 7 years, the feeling was near magical. Dr. Cole ran her hands through Tim's salt & pepper hair, pushing him further down towards her pussy. Her husband's gift was oral sex, and she'd craved it ever since his death.

Dr. Abel grabbed Shelly's curved hips, licking, biting and sliding down her soft belly. Heading under her skirt, he started from thighs upward again. He began biting upon her soft flesh, giving her pussy chills. With every conquered inch, Tim could smell Shelly's sweet arousal calling him forward. She was so wet, her lust stained white panties.

Arriving at her sweet slit, Tim engulfed the wet cloth with his mouth. Wringing the wet crotch with his lips, Shelly's love juice trickled onto his tastebuds. Using his teeth, he yanked downward. Snapping her waistbands, he tossed Shelly's panties away.

He lunged for her sopping folds. Burying his face within pink satin, he drank Shelly's fine wine. Aged to perfection, he let her feminine juice saturate his mouth. Rising upward, he sucked on her swollen clit. Shelly shook in moments, forced into near instant orgasm. She'd craved it so long, it had been awaiting release.

Dr. Abel pulled his pants down, still fully buckled. His throbbing 8-inches of steel sprang out. The blond therapist reached for it, wrapping her hands upon it like a blind woman touching sight itself. Feeling it again was like rediscovering life.

She led Tim forward, aligning him with her soft hole. He sank inside her creamy red lips. The sensation was surreal to them both. Although Shelly had fingered herself since losing her husband, such length and girth was foreign to her.

Crying out in painful pleasure, she spread her legs in an upward V. Tim rammed all 8-inches inside her at once. They both let out deeply satisfied moans, as if finding an oasis in the desert of life.

It was as if Shelly was Tim's first woman since losing his wife. His balls spanked her thick ass cheeks, her smooth legs wrapped around Tim's muscular ass. He crashed into her with desperate need. It was rough, hard, passionate sex, though it was also loving.

They found the best of both worlds. Shelly moaned with each new impaling. She absorbed every stretching blow, tingling with newfound arousal. The feeling inside her was of lost virginity.

The drunk driver's bloody wounds seeped. Gagged and tied, he was helpless. All he could do was watch his captors fuck. Tim looked up at Mike. It was something much greater than sex to Dr. Abel; it was a declaration of victory. While the drunk took the doctor's life away, it was in his enemy's presence that Tim won it back.

Returning his gaze to Shelly, Tim pounded her hard like a wildling. The blond's tight pussy milked Tim's cock, begging for his cum. She didn't expect to get pregnant at 40, nor was she sure if it'd be wise. Though a part of her needed it.

One hard thrust after another, Tim returned to Shelly's soft lips. With a deep, passionate tongue kiss, he exploded inside the curvy therapist. Breaking the kiss, both cried out in lust. Tim's manly moan was more grunt-like. Shelly's cry was high-pitched, feminine, and tearful. With each load, more salty drops sailed down her cheeks. They weren't tears of sadness, but of joy.

Her legs wrapped tighter around the doctor's ass. Her hands roved his strong, sweat-covered back, feeling his body twitch with every new load. Tim flooded Shelly's sweet pussy. The feeling alone made Shelly shutter in another orgasm. Her tight pussy got tighter, choking every bit of cum from Dr. Abel's thick cock.

Tim's shout echoed through the house. He broke down in tears again. For the first time in a decade, the aching pain of loss was gone. He felt alive. Lowering his head into Shelly's breasts, they both let relief flow like liquid love.

They stayed like that for a good 10 minutes, rising like the reborn. After dressing, they looked over at the gas soaked, battered prisoner. "What are you gonna do with him?" Shelly asked.

Fear danced in Mike's eyes. For the first time ever, the arrogant prick was humbled to the point of real tears. With match in-hand, Tim approached the shaking prisoner. Striking the match on a dry part of Mike's face, Tim waved it in front of him.

The gag was removed, as the drunk driver shouted, "I'm sorry, man! I'm fucking sorry, I really mean it this time. Let me go...I don't wanna die...I'll do anything to save myself. I won't say a word to the cops...I'll tell my wife this was a random robbery. She doesn't even know about my DUI...doesn't know I hit your wife at all!"

"No...you won't tell your wife it was random."

"Why not?"

Tim removed the letter from his pocket. The drunk driver's eyes opened wide, doctor cracked a wicked smile. "Hand me the scalpel," he said to Shelly. Still in a whirl of sex, she retrieved it from the bag, handing it over without question.

"What the hell you gonna do with that?" Mike shouted.

"You won't have to tell your wife what you did," Tim said, placing the court-ordered letter on the drunk driver's shoulder. Dr. Abel plunged the thin blade into it, pinning the letter to his prisoner. "She'll read about it in your own words."

Mike screamed in horrid pain. The doctor knew exactly where to stab, assuring the greatest pain, yet allowing him to live. Tim followed with a hard fist to the head, knocking the enemy unconscious.

"What if he tells?" Shelly asked in worry.

"He won't."

"Why not?"

"Because...he'll never forget me again."

*****

Darcy hugged her stepfather tightly. As awkward as she expected it to be, it wasn't. *It's kinda strange...but I actually feel more comforted, closer to him than ever. I hope he feels the same when I flat out ask him if he knocked me up. I'll do it...nicer than that, of course.*

As the hug broke, a big smile crossed Tim's face. "Congratulations, my red rose."

"You look...different."

"I'm proud."

"Like a father?" she asked, needing an actual confirmation.

He gently nodded, "Like a father," he said passionately.

"I just needed to hear you say it...for sure. But you know...this is Sean's baby. It has to be."

"It is. That's why I did it...for you both. I couldn't be more proud to be a grandfather. I was just the sperm donor...donated a little different than my usual procedure."

Phew, Darcy exhaled. "Thank you for that. Thank you for everything, stepdad." She hugged him again, feeling his love for her. Upon breaking the hug, the same beaming smile stared back. "It's more than pride. That look on your face...in your eyes...it's something else...I can tell."

The newly made man blushed, staring downward. "You know me too well, stepdaughter."

"You met someone."

"She's actually my therapist."

"Isn't that like...illegal?"

"Unethical...not illegal. And let's be honest...who am I to judge ethics?"

"Good point," she said. "So, you're...a couple?"

"We've yet to define it...who knows what the future holds? I just know...I feel alive again. Creating life was the answer. A piece of me...a piece of your mother...via you. It's like...bringing her back," he said. "Balancing the world...with one good soul to offset the bad ones."

A tear rolled down Darcy's cheek. Tim wiped it away, as a tear ran down his own. Darcy did the same to him. "There's one thing I have to ask, stepdad. I'm sorry to do it..."

"I'm going to tell him," he interrupted.

"How'd you know what I was gonna ask?" Darcy asked.

"Because...a family is built on truth...not lies. We owe it to Sean."

Worry painted Darcy's face. "Do you think he'll try to kill us?"

"No."

"You're more confident than I am," she said. "How will you go about it? An alpha thing?"

"No...a family thing."

*****

Tim and Sean Abel sat down at a bar, two beers in-hand. "Cheers," Tim said clinking glasses with his son.

Sean suspiciously clinked back. He watched his father sip the bitter brew. "OK dad, what's wrong?"

"Nothing. Can't a father and son meet for a drink...talk family...family business?"

"You're no drinker...and a bar is as foreign to you as a strip club. Put down the beer and spill your mind."

Tim paused, trying to force the words out. Instead, he sucked down the whole glass of beer. After cringing, he called to the bartender, "I think I need another."

Watching in impressive disbelief, Sean lifted his glass. "After you finally say what you can't seem to say...I may need another as well. Actually, bartender...make it a boilermaker," Sean said, sucking down his glass of beer.

"Make that two boilermakers," Tim joined.

"Uh...dad...not a good idea."

The bartender brought two more beers. He dropped a shot glass of whiskey into the brew. Foaming like a witches' cauldron, it looked quite dangerous to Tim's eyes. He watched Sean drink it straight, catching the shot glass in his mouth afterward.

"You're probably right about *that*, son," he said, pushing the drink away.

"Come on, dad...just spit it out already."

After another long nervous pause, Tim quickly blurted out, "I impregnated Darcy." Panic filled him, as he felt like a son about to be punished. Unable to look at Sean's reaction, Tim grabbed the boilermaker, sucking down the strong brew. Catching the cup in his mouth, he gagged the glass back into the mug. "My God! What's wrong with you? Drinking that poison?"

Sean smirked. "Now that's the father I recognize."

Tim was shocked. He expected his son to go on a rampage. "Did you hear what I said *before* the drink? I *seeded* her!"

"I heard what you said...and I already knew."

"Darcy told you? You're not fuming at the mouth? I drugged..."

Sean held up his hand, "I don't wanna know any damn details. I'd prefer to picture a test-tube...nothing more."

"I can gladly omit details."

"Darcy told me."

"I told her I'd confess."

"She didn't tell me about you...her pregnancy."

"Then what did she tell you?"

Sean paused, thinking back to Darcy's words. "She told me about a certain day...months ago. She found you standing at a gravestone."

"It feels like just yesterday."

"You who told her, 'You belong with a Dr. Abel...just not me.' You told her...we deserved to be together...she belonged with me...not you."

"And I was right, son. I let *my* pain, *my* hurt, *my* selfishness cloud my fatherly judgment. I failed you during those days. And to be honest, I feared I might've failed you now."

"But you got it right in the end...*then* and *now*. Am I happy I couldn't knock up my wife? No. But I'm grateful you risked everything...to help us."

"I did. I love you both...willing to do anything to save you...from the life and pain I lived. Tell me though, honestly...how'd you really know?"

"I'm a doctor, dad."

"And a damn good one...in case I haven't told you before."

Sean was shocked, having never heard his father say it. The senior doctor was hard on Sean throughout, intent on making his son the best doctor he could be. "Well, I may not be an OBGYN...T," Sean smirked, "But I've given my share of disappointing diagnosis. Incurable cancer, rare diseases...so on. When you called with the news...your tone said it all. It *was* my fault."

"Son, it's not a case of fault! It's a case of biology...nothing you could do!"

"I know...I know. I also know...you were trying to protect me from my macho-self...an impossible task. You wanna know the truth? If I had to choose anyone's sperm to fill in for mine...you'd be the man."

A humbled Tim hugged his son. As the hug broke, Tim yelled, "Bartender, two more boilermakers."

"Dad?"

"What the hell...you only live once."

*****

9 Months Later

A full-term, round-bellied Darcy waddled into her stepfather's exam room. Sean accompanied her. The redhead changed into her gown, sitting in the chair. Having carried full-term, she was expected to go into labor at any moment.

"Let's do it," Sean said with a devious look in his eyes.

"What? Here? Now? Stepdad can walk in on us!" Darcy exclaimed.

"Has any doctor ever come in immediately? Trust me...we take our time."

She paused, having been extra horny during her gestational period. "I may regret this...but...take me!" she said, giving in to raging hormones.

"Just like we pretended...on our honeymoon," Sean said, snapping on rubber gloves. "But this fantasy...will come true." He lowered the gyno chair. Darcy's back lay flat, her feet were raised in stirrups. The redhead's gown fell open, swollen pregnant belly and breasts heaved upward towards the heavens. Her red pubic hair had grown back in full, fiery as a burning bush. Legs spread wide, the patient's pink slit was on full display.

Stepbrother Sean removed his clothes, revealing cut abs, strong legs and arms, a model-like body. The dark-haired doctor put on a white medical jacket. He followed by administering the stethoscope to his neck. His 7-inch cock protruded from the coat's open part, pointing right for her pussy. He inhaled, following Darcy's arousal home.

Sliding his cock along her slit, he entered with ease. The exam room door suddenly opened. Darcy gasped.

It was Dr. Tim Abel. He let out a gasp as well. "I'm sorry," he said, turning to leave.

"No, Dad...stay," Sean said.

"Excuse me?" Tim asked.

"Yeah...excuse you?" Darcy questioned in shock.

"She belongs to us both...at least...one *last* time," he said with sincerity in his voice. "We'll examine her...in every intimate way."

Darcy and her stepfather shared shocked gazes. Without a word spoken, Tim frantically removed his clothes. Also opting to keep on his jacket only, his 8-inch cock sprang out of it. He snapped on gloves too, approaching his pregnant stepdaughter with lustful desire.

Oh shit! It's just like what I imagined on our wedding night...in my head! Darcy thought.

Dr. Tim Abel removed the medical tape, wrapping his stepdaughter's wrists. Tossed to Sean, the younger doctor taped his stepsister's ankles. Stepfather Tim went straight for Darcy's mouth. His manly arrow aimed for her lips. She opened on command, swallowing his thick rod. Offering no pause, he sank into an immediate deep throat. The pregnant redhead took every inch without a single gag, thanks to stepfather's expert teaching.

Sean watched his father's eyes roll upward in pleasure, as he fucked Darcy's soft mouth. The stepbrother drove into his stepsister's pussy, holding onto her thick thighs. He pounded her, balls-deep. Dual sensations tingled Darcy's body.

The senior doctor roved Darcy's breasts with a latex touch. Over the 9 months, they swelled from C-cup to D. His large expert hands massaged and squeezed the massive mammaries like water balloons. Suddenly, he reached over to the nearby drawer. With cock remaining in stepdaughter's mouth, he removed two small rubber bands and two forceps clamps. Although the bands were often used for hemorrhoid tying, it was clear Dr. Abel had something different in mind.

Tossing one to Sean, father and son stretched the medical bands around Darcy's breasts. Then, they twisted the ends so they bubbled, growing another cup size. Pausing a moment, Darcy freed her mouth, moaning from the pressure. Tim grabbed a handful of red hair, forcing her mouth back onto his slippery throbbing cock.

With both medical bands in place, they clamped Darcy's puffed aureoles. The forceps' mouths clamped from the sides. Darcy moaned in painful pleasure, feeling like her breasts would explode. Sensitive nerves within the nipple were stimulated, milk ducts were primed. It was milk Tim had a craving for.

Stepfather Tim Abel grabbed a nipple, beginning a tugging motion. His face tightened, feeling his stepdaughter's mouth tighten around his thick cock. Sean reached for the opposite nipple, jerking it even harder. Darcy's pussy also tightened, making Sean grit his teeth.

The pregnant redhead moaned through the cock gag. Both men fucked her holes harder, milking her nipples more aggressively. They kept it up, fighting their own releases, eager to free the expecting mother of her breast milk. Their latex pinch combined with the rubber bands and clamps. Darcy's breasts turned a slight shade of purple, red tips tingled with fire.

A tiny droplet of clear liquid appeared, proving they'd struck gestational gold. Tim Abel positioned his head down to Darcy's engorged breasts. Wanting to taste his wife, Sean leaned in to suck the other. They drank the rising liquid like concrete through straws.

The men bit on the tender tips like rare prime rib. Soon, ecstasy seeped from her nipple like a calcium fountain.

Darcy wanted to shout, feeling stinging pressure tingle her tits. However, she was forced to accept more of her stepfather and stepbrother. A breast induced orgasm trickled through her body. Although not quite as powerful as a vaginal or clitoral explosion, it teased her just right.

Having drank their fill of their step-kin, the men returned to upright positions. With one hand pumping Darcy's red hair, Tim gently grabbed his stepdaughter's throat, removing it just as quick.

"Choke her," Sean said, handing over the stethoscope to his father.

"She's pregnant...it's...not a very good..."

"She wants this...*badly*," he said.

Darcy's head bobbed in agreement, still sucking away at her stepfather's hard cock. Tim excitingly wrapped the cord around her tender neck. Starting aggressively, he pulled hard, restricting air from her windpipe. Darcy immediately felt the pressure build in her head. Tim was impressed that his stepdaughter went from an inexperienced virgin to sexual freak in mere months.

His squeeze got harder, as Darcy's mouth opened, gasping desperately for air. He quickly gagged her deeper with a bulbous head. Sailing across her flailing tongue, he plugged her throat.

Sean continued driving into his stepsister's soaked pussy. Her sweet juices were spackled all over his balls and thighs, running down his muscular legs. He watched Darcy's face match her hair, beet red. The step-doctor got more aroused seeing his wife's arms and legs struggle to break free of her tape-bond. He knew dark pleasure was accompanying it.

Stepfather and stepbrother pounded away with alpha vigor, fucking Darcy's mouth and pussy. A fan of sexual asphyxiation anyway, Darcy's pregnant hormones increased the taboo pleasure. The more she gasped, the tighter Tim choked her with the stethoscope.

Finally, Darcy broke. Her curved body shook in captivity, grinding into the reclined gyno seat. Both her pussy and mouth tightened around the dual step-cocks. She felt her stepfather's balls smack her face, stepbrother's balls smack her curvy ass. Dizzy flutters filled Darcy's mind, rounded body heaved in fits of electric orgasm.

Pushed to the edge of consciousness, her pleasure was heightened when both men erupted inside her. Stepfather erupted first, firing a hot load into her warm wet mouth. The sweet and savory seed sailed into her throat, flooding so furiously, she could barely swallow it fast enough.

Then came the gush of stepbrother sperm into Darcy's pregnant pussy. Although not as virile as his father's, Sean's delivery was fuller. He kept firing like a cum cannon, his stepsister was the battlefield.

Filled from both ends, Darcy lay captive to their dominance. The young girl basked in sacred submission to the men she loved. After firing their last loads, they withdrew. A white ring remained around both sets of feminine lips.

Both step-doctors gazed at each other, neither ready to quit. With one nod, they moved into further action. Darcy's wrist and feet bindings were cut free, nipple bands and clamps removed.

To her surprise, Tim grabbed Darcy's top, Sean her bottom. They carried their pregnant kin toward the adjacent exam table. Their hold was tight, step rushed. The bubble-bellied redhead felt like a piece of meat. She loved it.

Sean took full control, transferring his wife into a cradle carry. Her arms wrapped around his neck. She gazed lovingly at him, no words needed. He'd already sacrificed so much for her happiness and she appreciated it. Of course, he wasn't done yet.

Dr. Tim Abel lay on the paper-lined exam table, fully erect again. Sean sat Darcy down on her stepfather's 8-inch weapon, letting her gently sink into a cowgirl position. Completely hard again as well, Sean climbed up on the table. Positioning himself behind her, he buried his face in her asshole. Darcy's stepbrother licked the puckered hole as his father pumped his wife.

Once the asshole was lubed, Sean grabbed his stepsister's curvy hips, holding her still. Placing his bulbous head to her asshole, he impaled her from behind. The pregnant redhead cried out in a deep feminine moan. Her body went completely limp, fully submitting her holes to the step-doctors.

For a moment, it felt like she'd tear in two. However, Sean was slow and careful, letting his bulbous head penetrate the tight anal ring. With one pop, he was inside his stepsister's ass. After sinking deeper into her secret garden, father and son rhythmically fucked her in double-penetration.

Darcy's luscious, life-filled curves swayed with the entrance of each step-offering. Her body was pushed beyond physical, emotional, and mental limits. One moment it was harsh pain, then unreal pleasure. Her G-spot was squashed by two cocks, vaginal and anal nerves stimulated on and off.

Tim and Sean Abel's faces tensed in sexual anguish. Their joint invasion crowded every inch of the pregnant patient. The tightness nearly burst their cocks. As Darcy placed her hands on stepfather Tim's white-coated chest, she rocked back and forth, shifting her full body weight. Each cock was milked to a straining point.

Feeling cum rise, both men couldn't fight it anymore. Sean was the first to erupt inside his stepsister's ass. Streams of hot cum coated Darcy's anal avenue. The sticky, squishy inner-feeling pushed her further off the sexual cliff.

Next, stepfather Tim blasted his stepdaughter's pussy with a life-giving load. Yet again, Darcy was cream-filled in two orifices by her step-doctors. Suddenly, a shout escaped her, entire body shifting and shaking like the deepest quake.

Every curve on her trembled, breath huffed and puffed. She'd never felt such a pleasure-rush strike her at once. It was like every orgasm she'd ever had, combined into one tidal wave.

Her body pushed so hard, she squirted G-spot fluid all over her stepfather's cock. In the midst of squirting one end, her swollen strained nipples fired another type of squirt. New streams of breast milk baptized stepfather Tim's chest and face.

As her last wave of orgasm swept over, Darcy crashed upon her stepfather, Sean sandwiched her. After a moment of sweaty quiet, she started moaning again. "Another orgasm?" Sean asked, realizing her cry sounded different.

"No...Sean...I think I'm having the baby! Like...right now!"

"The sex...induced her!" Tim realized. "Her water must've broke with the squirt! Couldn't have happened in a better place."

"Or with a better doctor. Are you ready to deliver my child, Dr. Abel?" Sean said, as both men withdrew from Darcy's holes.

"I'm ready," Tim said with conviction.

"Then to the hospital we go."

*****

"It's a girl!" Dr. Tim Abel shouted, holding up a healthy child. The umbilical cord was cut. Dried and nasally squeegeed, she was placed in Darcy's arms. The redhead cried as her stepbrother and stepfather joined her in joy.

"She's amazing!" Sean declared. "I just realized we never discussed names."

Both Darcy and Tim connected gazes. "*Debra* Abel," they jointly announced, honoring the woman taken from them years ago. Tim's pain was not only gone, but for the first time since losing his wife, his heart was officially healed.

"I want you to meet someone," Tim said, motioning his nurse to bring someone in.

Everyone waited in wonderment. Shelly Cole entered, her warm smile greeting them all. "Hello," she said. "I'm Shelly, nice to meet you both."

"The *therapist*," Darcy said.

"Yes," Tim told her. "Though now...you can call her...my woman," he said in pride.

"Actually...there's a new title," Shelly informed him.

"Really?" Tim asked in surprise. "What is it?"

"Baby-mama," Shelly said with a smirk.

Greater shock filled Tim's face. "You're pregnant? We did it?"

"We did," she said, finally free from her own pain. For the first time, she also found the cure to losing love, losing life. It was giving birth to new love, new life.

"Come on, everyone...a hug," Tim said, all four embraced around the new child.

"Here's to step-family," Darcy said.

"No." Tim corrected her. "Here's to family."

.

Other Books by J.D. Grayson

More titles available on Amazon

All books are now available in Paperback. For autographed copies please send your request to JDGrayson@hotmail.com

THE STEP DOCTORS
Available at: Amazon

Darcy Smith enters her stepfather's medical practice. Expecting to see the usual female physician, Dr. Sean Abel arrives instead. The 30 year-old stepbrother dares to break his father's rule, forbidden from examining the girl. Thrust into a living-taboo, the step-doctor intimately explores the girl he was raised with.

Learning of the insubordination, Dr. Tim Abel disciplines his son. However, the stepfather questions his own hidden fantasies, enticing him to break his own rules. As Darcy comes to enjoy it, an unthinkable decision arises. Could she fall in love with her step-doctors? More importantly, could she actually choose between the two of them?

*****

YOUR FRIENDLY NEIGHBORHOOD BDSM CLUB
Available at: Amazon

After entering the local PTA meeting, Caroline Chase feels out of place. She finds an unwelcoming bunch of ladies, prim and proper in every manner. Owen Hayes, the dapper PTA president, presents the same air of perfection. Too good to be true, she knows the most polished people often hide the dirtiest secrets.

Intrigued by the group's plastic facade, Caroline Chase returns again. It's then, she finds a reality which only existed in her sexual fantasies. Challenged to submit, she'll be forced to face questions of inner strength and willpower. However, Caroline will soon discover, she's not the only one in need of an awakening.

*****

THE PREGNANCY TRANCE
Available at: Amazon

Amber Evans enters a hypnotherapist's office seeking help. Unable to get pregnant, she's desperate to find an answer. Eager to cure her, Bruce Carson examines her subconscious mind, treading a darker path than he expected to walk.

Fighting his own battle of darkness, Bruce hopes redemption lies in Amber's cure. Though to heal her, he'll have to survive the dangerous place it takes him. Obsessed with his mission, he'll even risk his life to deliver the pregnancy trance.

*****

MARRIAGE THERAPY:
A DOM, A SUB & A CUCKOLD
Available at: Amazon

Lori and Tyler Hale have a nice home, good jobs, and decent relationship. Though while Tyler is happy to forego bedroom matters, Lori desires a kinky edge. With no answer in sight, the couple turns to marriage therapy.

Recommended by a friend, Dr. Stone welcomes the couple into his office. The Hales soon discover their therapist's unique way of treatment. Using the tools of sexual discipline, he pushes their marriage to the edge. Willing to risk their breaking, he challenges their sexual limits. Though the more he explores his female patient, the more he's tempted to let them fail.

*****

THE FANTASY FACTORY: EDGY ROLE PLAY
Available at: Amazon

Vicky Lane's sex life has hit a wall. Failing to spice things up with sexy outfits and toys, the luscious housewife threatens her husband with an affair. After he carelessly dares her to go forward, Vicky calls Gavin's bluff. Raising the stakes, she lets her dark side shine.

She signs up for the fantasy factory, where fantasy becomes reality. Wanting to act out her darkest taboo, she signs her freedom away, putting it in the hands of unknown men. Taken at random, an edgy adventure follows suit. Vicky hopes to teach Gavin a lesson of her value, though by the end, the lesson will belong to them both.

The Fantasy Factory series will be an occasional series of non-sequential, "Paid for hire" role-play. They can be read in any order.

*****

DOCTOR MÉNAGE
Available at: Amazon

Returning to their hometown in style, Doctors Mason & Ross open a sexual medicine practice. Blessed with wealth and good looks, the bachelors are desired by every female in the zip code. Since the girls can't win the doctors' hearts, they must settle for sexual treatment instead.

Attending their high-school reunion, the doctors are approached by a face from their past. The popular and beautiful Kayla Carter seeks them out, hoping they'll cure her sexual dysfunction. Agreeing to treat her, the two doctors make a deal to stimulate her body, but not their hearts. Of course, promises are easier to make than keep.

*****

THE COLONY:
ARRIVAL (PART I)
TEMPTATION (PART II)
PROPHECY (PART III)
ADDICTS (PART IV)
Available at: Amazon, Smashwords, iBooks & B&N

After years of marital heartache, Dylan & Alexa Hunter have lost the will to go on. After being approached by a mysterious man, they are offered a chance to start over in a utopian paradise. The word eternity is spoken, though left undefined.

On the island of Aionios, no fruit is forbidden, no pleasure denied. Accepting the tempting offer, the couple surrenders everything, including freewill itself. Though they'll soon learn that even paradise has a dark side.

*****

SLAVES & BREEDERS:
ABDUCTED INTO SEX SLAVERY (PART I)
CHOSEN TO BREED (PART II)
INTO THE FIRE (PART III)
Available at: Smashwords, iBooks & B&N

Having grown up in foster care, Haley White only knows disappointment. Cloaked in a mask of false strength, the troubled teen enters a world of harsh reality. As she attempts to better her life, few opportunities open their door to her.

As the years tick by, the 21-year old discovers an ad for a modeling agency. Tired of working small jobs for small money, she agrees to a photo shoot. After being chosen for the position, her fate takes a frightening turn. Haley White is abducted.

Taken to a remote island, she's an immediate candidate to breed her new master's heir. However, her rebellious attitude will have to be broken first. Feeling helpless in her captivity, she finds that her captor shares a common bond.

*****

THE PATIENT:
PHYSICAL (PART I)
DOUBLE DOSE (PART II)
THE CURE (PART III)
Available at: Amazon, B&N, iBooks, Smashwords, KOBO, Sony, and Diesel

Twenty-two year old, Rebecca Stone is a naive girl with medical anxiety. Having minimal sexual experience, and being submissive in nature, she is prime meat in the hands of horny predators. Sensing her obvious weakness, her new boss demands a pre-employment physical. However, what she doesn't know, is that the doctor's secretly working with him, exploiting timid girls like herself.

Rebecca is forced to face her deep fear of doctors, pulled into a world of medical submission. Along the journey, she will discover the root of her feelings, and gain a newfound fetish in the process.

*****

TEACHING EMMA:
A CONTRACT OF SUBMISSION (PART I)
THE MASTER/SUB EXPERIENCE (PART II)
FREEDOM OF SUBMISSION (PART III)
Available at: Amazon, Smashwords, iBooks & B&N

Emma Heart starts college with an unusual elective: Human Sexuality-Fetish and Lifestyles. She doesn't know that her new teacher, Mark Ryan, is as unusual as the course itself. The class is given a contract of submission, agreeing to become his subs, empowering him their Dom. The lessons that follow will not be learned from books, but bodies.

As he focuses on Emma, Professor Ryan begins to question his own methods. Feeling stronger for his student than expected, he realizes the only outcome is heartbreak. He must decide between love or scholastic duty. The question is...can he?

*****

THE HYPNOTIST: SEX TRANCE
Available at: Amazon

Hoping to cure his wife's bedroom boredom, Sean Day turns to hypnotherapist, Joseph Ryan, to cure his wife. Though, due to Misty's uptight upbringing, the hypnotist is forced to skirt the rules. He lies to her.

Under the guise of smoking addiction treatment, Misty is seduced into trance. Joseph intends to fix her intimacy issues. However, after exploring Misty's dark mind, a deeper issue is revealed. Her words unlock Mr. Ryan's own unspoken fetish, forcing him to break new ground. Pushed to the edge of submission, Mrs. Day will face her shameful secrets, along with the mental bonds that hold her captive.

THE DENTIST: SEDATION
Available at: Amazon

Throughout Dr. Ivy's life, a dark fantasy has tested his limits of self-control. Finally ready to cross the threshold of reality, the allure of exploiting sedated patients claims him. As satisfying as the experience turns out, it fails to cure a lonely heart.

Realizing he requires more than a warm body, the doctor revisits an abandoned idea. Working on numerous formulas, he discovers that the right mix of nitrous oxide will make his dream come true.

Just when his plans are in place, a new regulation forces him to hire a dental assistant. The beautiful Kimberly Carter arrives, watching his every move. It appears his fantasy-driven dreams are thwarted, when he discovers his assistant may share them as well.

About J.D. Grayson

All books are now available in Paperback. For autographed copies please send your request to JDGrayson@hotmail.com

Website: www.JDGraysonBooks.com
Twitter: @JDGraysonBooks
Facebook: http://www.facebook.com/JDGraysonBooks

You can contact J.D. Grayson at JDGrayson@hotmail.com

J.D. Grayson lives in the state of Florida, where the heat and sweat naturally lead him to write erotica. Preferring short erotica to long form, he tries to offer a burst of pleasure, while merging an interesting story with a few twists along the journey.

With every work, Grayson attempts to straddle the line of sensuality and kink, story and sex, as well as fantasy and reality. Although sex always leads the way, he strives to add imagination to every plot line, in addition to each sex act. Some stories are lighter in tone; others are darker, though he always aims for a tasteful presentation.

His ultimate goal is to add spice to the life of readers. In his daily conversations with "average couples," he discovered that the current state of sexuality is not in a good place. Somehow, it's been lost in maddening schedules, busy lives, and shamed stereotypes. Its importance and priority are pushed to the back burner, as a chore not a reliever.

If just one of his stories adds some lust to their love, then his mission is accomplished.